# FURTHER STORIES FROM THE OLD SILK ROAD

# FURTHER STORIES FROM THE OLD SILK ROAD

RETOLD BY ERIC CHEETHAM
ILLUSTRATED BY ROBERTA MANSELL

EDITED BY STEVE AND ROBERTA MANSELL

THE BUDDHIST SOCIETY

*For Jean and Chip, John and Pat*

*A Note on the Cover:* Hsuan-tsang, the figure on the front cover of the book, was an important Chinese monk and pilgrim who was one of the four great translators of Buddhist Sanskrit texts into Chinese. In the seventh century, Hsuan-tsang spent 16 years on pilgrimage to India, travelling there and back on the Old Silk Road. He was the famous 'Tripitaka' of the Monkey stories. The cover illustration is based on traditional images of him.

Published by The Buddhist Society
Patron: His Holiness the Dalai Lama
Registered Charity No. 208677

First published 2015


Publication supported by The Hokun Trust



ISBN: 978 0 901032 44 7

A catalogue record for this book is available from the British Library

Edited by Sarah Auld
Original design concept by Roberta Mansell
Artistic Direction by Jonny Templeton
Photography by James Newell
Designed by Avni Patel

Printed in China by Toppan Leefung

**THE BUDDHIST SOCIETY**
58 Eccleston Square
London
SW1V 1PH
T: 020 7834 5858
E: info@thebuddhistsociety.org
thebuddhistsociety.org

Once Upon a Time

# CONTENTS

# PUBLISHER'S FOREWORD

When the Buddha spoke, it was to audiences that came from very different walks of life, from all strata of society – kings and princes, brahmins, warriors and working men and women – from different provinces, speaking different dialects. Directness and simplicity were the hallmarks of his teaching. His capacity to speak to the deepest part of the human being marked out his teachings from that of other teachers of the time.

It was said that regardless of language, all who heard the Buddha understood what he was saying. Clearly it was not just the words that moved the hearts of those who heard him, but something about his whole presence – his generosity of spirit, his strength and energy, simplicity, gentleness and warmth, and his true understanding of human nature – that so deeply affected his audience.

No matter how subtle, erudite or detailed it is, no formalised teaching can convey the essence of spirit that is beyond words and doctrinal formulations.

The stories compiled here in this volume, from the Buddha's great way, point towards a life that lies beyond mere words.

This book, written by Eric Cheetham and so beautifully illustrated by Roberta Mansell will interest all those on a spiritual path, no matter their religious or cultural background, as the stories within speak to all.

**Desmond Biddulph, President, The Buddhist Society, London, 2015**

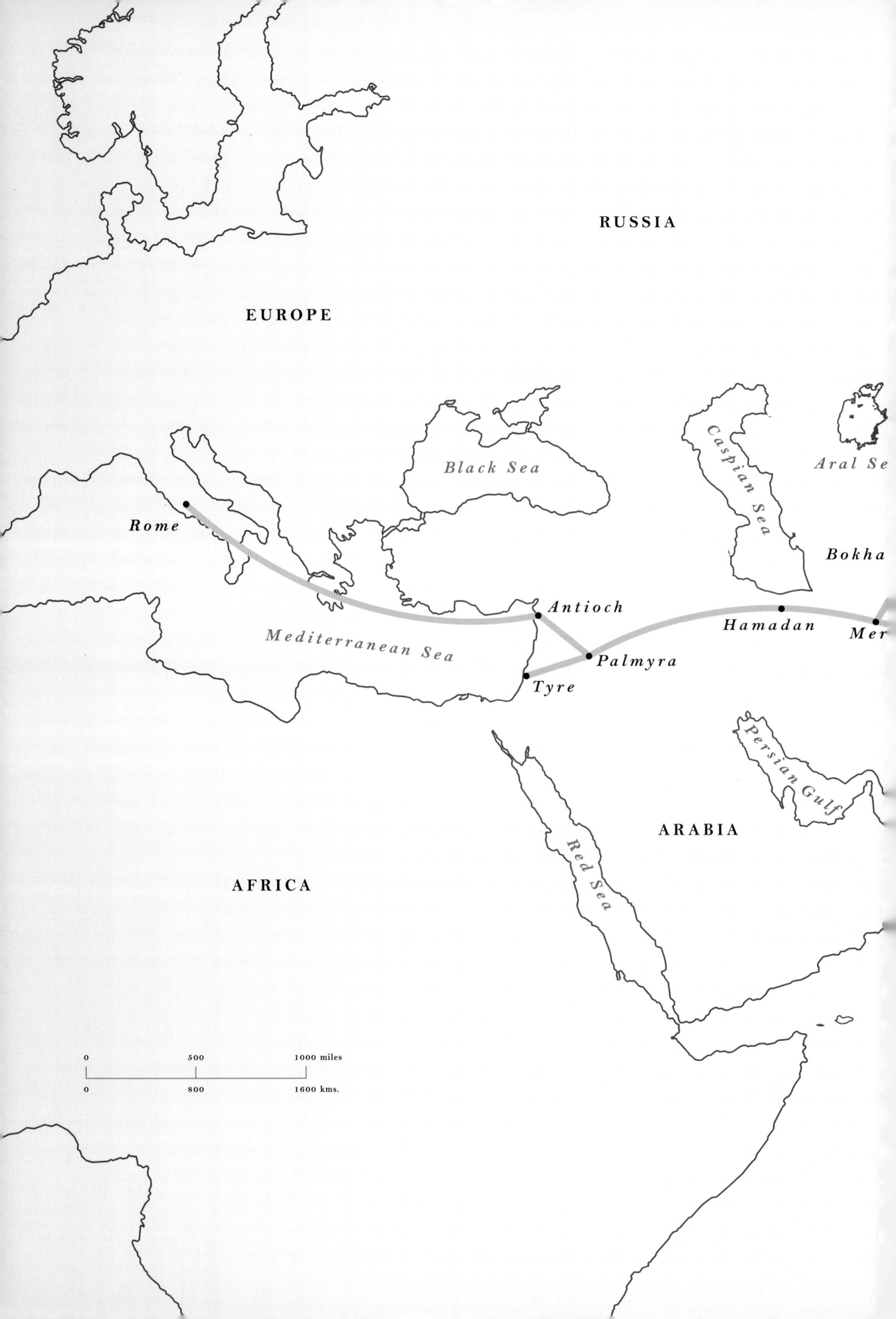
RUSSIA
EUROPE
Black Sea
Caspian Sea
Aral Se
Rome
Bokha
Antioch
Mediterranean Sea
Hamadan
Mer
Palmyra
Tyre
Persian Gulf
ARABIA
Red Sea
AFRICA
0
500
1000 miles
0
800
1600 kms.

# THE OLD SILK ROAD

# FOREWORD

Storytelling is the art of transporting heart and soul to another place. It joins together the real and the unreal, the true and the false. Stories are greater than the sum of their parts – they are living things, which evolve with each retelling. Nuances and insight can arise in the storyteller as she or he recounts a timeworn tale. Story elements may or may not have happened in historical time but, either way, such narrations are a creative act. Although we tend to think of stories as fiction, this is not to say that they are untrue – far from it. A good storyteller creates the story as it is being told and the listener is part of the creative action.

Stories, by use of repetition of phrase and theme, enchant and engage the heart and can stir the depths, bringing about a change of heart or a different way of seeing the world and our place in it. The greatest stories can overturn self. As the audience engages with the tale they forget themselves and become the characters in the telling. The capacity of the listener as well as the timing of the telling governs the effect that a particular tale may possess. The joy and sorrow of the protagonists becomes the joy and sorrow of those listening in a 'participation mystique'.

The evocative power of a story works by the process of memory. Stories are funny or sad or strike us in some way because they can chime with our shared experiences. Sometimes a story can strike us deeply yet we have no personal recollection or experience to which it points. When this happens the response is at once novel, catching us by surprise, and yet strangely familiar. It is as if another deeper element of consciousness, having been asleep for so long, stirs slightly, remembering something as in a dream. It is to this deeper element that stories based on spiritual matters are directed.

This collection of tales, now in your possession are taken from a number of sources but mainly from the Buddhist sutras (holy scriptures). They have as their source the powerful insight of an extraordinary man who lived over 2,500 years ago. The power of such a vision bursts upon the world suddenly but can take a long, long time to unfold. On the surface these tales contain the very human virtues and vices with which we are all familiar. In some cases they may shock or disturb us but we must never lose sight of the originating insight of the Buddha, an insight that runs through them and expresses the Buddha's warmth and understanding of human nature in all its facets.

Eric Cheetham has spent many years translating, teaching and making known the great works of Buddhism to us here in the West. The challenging nature of the material of his usual work has required a scholarly voice, however in this book he has put down his scholar's pen and instead retells tales from the Buddhist scriptures using the storyteller's argot, inviting us to participate face to face.

Roberta Mansell has been illustrating, drawing and painting for much of her life and is currently engaged in illuminating one of the most famous Buddhist scriptures, the Lotus Sutra. She has created a fine series of accompanying illuminations to delight and engage us as we travel that well-worn route along the Old Silk Road.

**Martin Goodson, London, 2015**

# INTRODUCTION

Most of these stories have been drawn from the tales contained in Buddhist sutra texts. Others come from collections of legends in Chinese and Indian popular literature or from ancient commentaries on canonical material. All of them travelled at the Old Silk Road which ran between ancient China and North West India and through Central Asia during the first 500 years C.E. They travelled along it either as written texts being carried into China from India by Buddhist monk teachers or in the heads of Buddhist sutra specialists who were en route to China to avoid repeated invasions by the nomad hordes which ravaged their homeland.

In the course of time these stories became the stock-in-trade of itinerant storytellers, who journeyed with the caravans in both directions. They would entertain the travellers by retelling tales of this kind around the campfires in the desert wilderness or in the caravanserais.

Of course, when the tales were told by the storytellers they would be shorn of their scriptural context (unless told by monks) and the details would be embellished and embroidered in time-honoured fashion, although the essential point of the story was rarely lost in the telling.

Apart from the traditional mix of a hero's exploits and of wondrous events, these stories display an extraordinary degree of warmth and humour. It needs to be stressed that such humour is not part of the customary embellishment, it is an integral part of the original scriptural text. Humour of this kind in scripture is rarely to be found in the major religions other than Buddhism.

It is to be hoped that the reader will derive as much pleasure and gentle instruction from these stories as the writer did when finding them and retelling them to others.

In this second edition of stories from the Old Silk Road, some new ones have been included as well as original illustrations which add another dimension of interest and interpretation. For these illustrations, the co-author of this collection, Roberta Mansell, is profusely thanked.

**Eric Cheetham, Rothwell, 2013**

# THE PRINCE WHO SOUGHT THE CREST JEWEL

A long, long time ago, a most amazing infant was born or, more precisely, reborn into a royal Indian family. This wonderful child startled everyone because, among other things, he could speak perfectly from birth! His parents, the king and queen, were understandably delighted since they knew this talent to be one of the marks of a bodhisattva: a holy one, a future sage.

They listened with incredulous joy as their baby described his previous lives. They knew that this memory was also a bodhisattva mark. In his most recent one, he told them, it was his practice to give away absolutely everything he could: anything that came into his hands was immediately passed on to others who might need it. And, oh, while he was on the subject, would his new parents kindly acquaint him with the full extent of the kingdom's wealth? Every bit of it would be needed since the young prince intended to continue his practice!

The king and the queen were not in the least dismayed. So sincere was their joy in him that they put at his disposal great riches, and let him get on with his giving. But the king's subjects were not pleased: they could not understand why a prince would want to give away so much that should one day be his. Was he unbalanced or twisted in some way? Their puzzlement changed to mistrust and that changed to fear: when they saw him coming with his gifts of food or clothing or jewels, they soon took to hiding from him or running away.

Well, how can a saint carry on his holy practice of giving if no one will accept his gifts? The young bodhisattva came to know frustration and finally, in great distress, went in tears to his mother, the only person left who would have anything to do with him as all the others were scared to death. "Why am I treated like this, mother? I am not a demon! How is it that I frighten people so much? In all my previous existences I have always loved giving and I have surpassed everyone through my gifts!"

Ah, previous lives! The mother noted this and wondered if the populace would think differently of him if they heard about his sincere goodness. So she put it about that he was really giving out of the loving kindness of his heart and that, of course, he wasn't trying to do them harm. In time the people abandoned their fear and stopped running away.

Indeed, as this happened when the prince was still a child, by the time he had grown up, he had given away everything that he had! As fast as he got it, he gave it away. So there came a day when he found that he had nothing left to give. He went to his father, the king, and asked for more but his father said, "You can't go on like this, my boy: our treasury will soon be empty! It's all very well, this feeling that you must give to everyone, but the kingdom has to be maintained and you're not earning anything, are you?" When he dried his tears, the young man begged his father to help him find a way to keep on giving. He needed limitless wealth! The perturbed king decided to call a meeting of his council and put the problem to them.

"My son," said the king to his advisers, "is, I suppose, rather peculiar (but don't let him hear that I said that) in that he feels that he has to give, give, give. The trouble is that he needs massive wealth to do this and if he carries on as he's been doing, we'll all be paupers. Have you any ideas at all about how to find more wealth for him?"

After much racking of brains, one possibility was put forward: somewhere, someone thought, somewhere beyond the Great Sea, in the Naga Kingdom, there existed a fabulous jewel of immeasurable value. This priceless gem was thought to be a Cintamani, or Crest Jewel, in the crown of the Naga King himself. No one knew exactly where he was, nor indeed whether he'd part with it if he were found, but only his Crest Jewel could offer the limitless wealth needed by their bodhisattva prince.

When the prince heard about the Crest Jewel, he was elated. To his parents' horror, he declared

himself ready to leave immediately, ready to embark upon the Great Sea and to journey into the unknown to find the Naga King. They, however, pleaded with him not to risk his life: the Great Sea promised terrible danger, incalculable risks. "We might never see you again," they wailed. "Please take everything we have left, every coin in the treasury is yours! Just don't go. Stay here with us, please, please!" But no, he explained firmly, he couldn't do that. "Your treasury is very limited and my aspirations are unlimited. I want to gratify everyone in such a way that they have no more needs." In the end, the anguished parents saw that no matter what they said, he would go, so they gave consent.

The news got around that the young prince was preparing an expedition to hunt for the Cintamani. Scenting the chance to make a quick fortune, five hundred merchants and a large number of hangers-on also decided to go and a great boat was made ready. It was moored in the traditional manner, with seven ropes, cutting one rope on each of the last seven days before sailing.

As the last day approached, however, the prince realised that when the seventh rope was cut, he would be afloat on the Great Sea without any idea about where to go. So he called out to the crowd thronging the quayside, "Does anybody know where to go? Can anybody tell us where the Jewel is to be found?" An old blind man spoke up. He had crossed the Great Sea seven times and knew the way, but he could not go again. "If I go again," he said, "I will not return, I know that. And anyway I am blind, so I couldn't show you the route, could I?" But the prince was very determined. He told the old man that this quest was not for private gain but to share the Great Jewel with everyone in the kingdom, it was to satisfy their every need for ever. They talked about the Way, the religious Path, and finally the young man persuaded him that they had to work together. They were an obvious partnership; the old pilot knows where the Jewel is but can't get to it; the young bodhisattva can get to it but he doesn't know where it is! "You are a wise man," said the prince, "how can my aspiration be accomplished without your help? You can't refuse me!" Moved by this sincere fervour, the old man agreed. "Right," he said, "I will go with you but I will surely die. You must promise me that you will gather my remains and set them down on an island in the middle of the Great Sea, the Island of the Gold Sand." So it was agreed and the seventh rope was cut.

No sooner were they on the Sea when trouble started – fierce winds and towering waves, relentless rain, wild storms – but their first landfall was a beautiful little island which even at a distance glittered as if made of jewels. When they landed, they found that it was covered with precious stones. The merchants poured over the side, bags open, ready to gather up all they could, but the old man and the bodhisattva stood aside from the frenzy.

"Hey there," the merchants called out, "get busy! It's all here, what you've come for, just lying about. Why don't you pick it up?" "Because this is not what I've come for," the young prince replied. "I'm seeking the Cintamani. These jewels are of no consequence, their value is limited. I need unlimited wealth and only the Cintamani can give me that. You go ahead and gather what you want but not too much or the boat will sink!" The merchants scoffed, "We're not worried. You can get us home safely no matter what we bring, just make the right prayers!" And they went on eagerly sifting and picking.

The blind man turned to the prince. "These people will do us no good," he said. "We must devise a way to leave them. We'll take a small boat and head off on our own, just the two of us, and let them have the big ship. But," he added, "our way will be very hard. I know what we're heading into – real trouble and hardship – and at the end of the boat journey I am going to die. You're going to have to bury me before you can go any further." And it all happened just as he said it would. The journey in

their little boat was full of hazard. A terrible storm arose and they could barely stay afloat. Finally they were washed up against a steep cliff. Abandoning ship, they struggled up the cliff face, clinging on to roots and branches, the giant waves of the Great Sea crashing at the rocks far below. With the last of their strength, they reached the top and crawled to safety, then as he knew would happen, the old man died.

The prince buried his good friend and guide as he had promised, there on the Island of the Golden Sand. It was now his task to go on by himself, following the instructions given to him by the old man. So, for the next seven days he swam through deep water, for the next seven he walked through water up to his neck, for the next seven through water up to his hips, for the next seven through water up to his knees, and then for seven on mud. There he found spread before him a great field of blue lotuses. The fragile beautiful blooms were so tightly packed together that the prince said to himself, "How can I cross these lovely flowers without crushing them? Yet I must cross them. Ah, yes, the concentration on space!" Through this previously acquired skilled practice, he then lightened his body and walked for seven days across the blossoms without bruising so much as a single petal.

Then, however, at the edge of the lotus field, he found himself blocked by a vast mass of poisonous snakes, undulating and hissing. "Formidable creatures," he thought, "I must enter upon the concentration on goodwill." This he did until the snakes ceased their hissing. Their hostility subsiding, they raised up their heads all together to offer a steady surface for him to walk upon. So he walked safely across the sea of serpents for yet another seven days and there he saw his next challenge: a flashing, gleaming township, lights glinting from every side, a whole city made of jewels, seven different kinds of jewels, guarded all around by seven ditches brimming with poisonous snakes. It was the Naga Kingdom.

Three great Naga Protectors guarded the gates. They saw the prince approaching from a great

distance but even from afar they knew him for what he was, a bodhisattva. They knew this not only because they recognised the special physical marks borne by such a person, unique features that result from lifetimes of high spiritual attainment, but also because only a bodhisattva could have surmounted the obstacles on the path to the Naga Kingdom. So they subdued the snakes and allowed him to enter the palace of the Naga King. There, the king and queen were still in mourning, although their beloved son had died long before. As the bodhisattva prince approached, the queen cried out in joy. "My child! I know you are my child! Where have you been reborn? Tell me!" And the prince recognised them as his previous parents.

He told them that he had been reborn as the crown prince of a great kingdom in India but one which had both rich and poor. The poor people there, he told them, were unable to overcome the torments of cold and hunger, of sickness and disease, and his compassion for them required that he seek great wealth to give away. He had therefore come to the Naga Kingdom, braving fantastic dangers on the way, seeking a fabulous jewel, the Cintamani, said to be of unlimited value. Was it not here, in the place of his father? "Ah, yes," said the queen, "it is here but it is in the crown upon your father's head! I know he will give you all you want from his treasury, any amount of wealth, enormous riches, to take back to your present parents but the Cintamani, the very crest of his crown, I don't think he'll part with that." "But mother, my loving mother, it is not for ordinary riches from a treasury that I have overcome these fearsome obstacles. It has been for one purpose only: to find the Crest Jewel, the Cintamani, the only source of endless wealth. That is all I want and all I want to take." "Well," said the worried woman, "have a word with him yourself, you never know."

And so he did, and in the end his father gave him the Crest Jewel. He gave it for many reasons: joy in his son's return, admiration for his son's bravery, respect for his son's path – but he gave it only after trying to persuade him to stay in the Naga Kingdom. "What do you want to go back for? You'll have to risk all kinds of dangers to get there and, after all, we're your primary parents! We should have first call on you! There's no need for you to go all the way back again!" But the bodhisattva persisted. "Father, this is what I came for. I came only to get the Jewel and bring it back for all those poor people in India. You don't know how it is there, Father, living here in this wonderful place. The people where I now live are wretched and suffering. I wouldn't have come here at all if the Jewel weren't needed. There is no point in my having braved all those dangers unless I bring it back and use it for their benefit!"

The Naga King knew he was right but as he removed the Crest Jewel from his crown and gave it to his son, he imposed one condition. "Here you are, here is the Jewel but you must promise me the next time you are reborn it will be with your mother and me." The son respectfully gave his promise to return. The bodhisattva took the jewel and fastened it within the lining of his garments. He then turned back in the direction from which he had come and, now knowing the way perfectly, he flew there in less than the time needed for a strong man to bend his arm!

His human parents, the king and queen in India, were jubilant at his return. "Where is it? Where is it?" they demanded in excitement. "Did you get it?" The prince replied, "It's right here, safely in the lining of my clothing." "In the lining? How small it must be! How did it get such a big reputation?"

The bodhisattva then asked his parents to see that the town was thoroughly cleaned, inside and out, to burn perfumes and suspend banners, and to decree that the fast must be kept and the moral rules observed. On the next day, after all this was done, he set up a high mast in the centre of the town square and from it suspended the Crest Jewel. Its flashing brilliance, its great rays, could be seen by everyone in the vast crowds flooding the town to see what their prince had brought back from his journey. When they were all gathered in the square, now bathed in the radiance from the Jewel, the bodhisattva made this aspiration: "If I am to reach Buddhahood and deliver all beings, may this gem obey my wishes and cause all precious objects to appear. May it gratify to the very last the needs of all men!"

Immediately the words were spoken, the clear, beautifully blue sky darkened. A great cloud began to gather, it grew and grew until it burst, raining down upon the people all kinds of precious things. It rained down food, clothing, bedding, cushions, medicines, every last thing they needed. And until the end of that bodhisattva's life, that rain never stopped!

This story is taken from *The Commentary on the Great Perfection of Wisdom*.

# THE PAINTER KARNA

Once, in ancient India, there was a painter called Karna. He left his home in the Valley of the Swat and travelled to Taxila to find work as an artist on the public buildings there. Taxila was then the capital of Kashmir and the seat of the emperor's Viceroy: a very rich place with enough temples and palaces and so on to keep a painter painting for a very long time. Indeed, it was twelve years before Karna finished work. He was paid thirty ounces of gold for all his work, quite a large sum in those days, even for twelve years of painting.

Now Karna was free to return home, where he had left a wife and several children, so he bagged up his gold and set out. The journey home would take at least a week since Karna would go mostly on foot. Naturally, he stopped here and there for a night's rest. One night he found that a festival was underway in a little village on his route and he soon discovered that it was Kathina: a Buddhist festival day when lay people present the monks with their new bowls, clothing and bedding. Karna was himself a Buddhist but having been so busy of late just earning a living, he had no time to think about these religious festivals but here he was now in the middle of one! So he said to himself, "Why don't I just go along and have a look? Why not?" And this he did, and as he watched the townspeople giving their gifts to the monks, he was strangely moved by a desire to give something himself.

Suddenly he felt, "This is the time for me to do something I've never done before. This is the time!" So he approached one of the monks and said to him, "How much would it cost to feed all of the monks, the entire Sangha in this town, for one day?" Perhaps the monk had powers of special vision (not unusual in those times) and saw into Karna's bag. Perhaps he counted the gold pieces or perhaps he didn't, but his answer was, "It would take thirty ounces of gold." Karna, out of this feeling he had of wanting to give something special, because he had never given anything before, said, "Right! There's thirty ounces of gold to feed the Sangha!" and handed over all he had earned for twelve years of work. Of course, it was understood by Buddhists in those days, and perhaps even now, that the giving of such a gift was an act of extreme merit. So after the monks had been fed and the festival was over, Karna set off home feeling very warm and good inside about what he'd done.

When he reached his home village and his own house, he called out, "Here I am, dear, after twelve years!" So out came the wife, with all the children, and snapped, "About time, too! Where have you been all these years?" "I've been working hard," he said. "I've been working at Taxila and I've spent twelve years on the temples there." And she said, "Well, what have you brought?" He answered, "Oh, well, hmm. Well, dear, it's like this ..." and he told his wife that he'd given all the gold to the monks at the previous town. She was livid! She went absolutely spare. "Here am I slaving my fingers to the bone and there you are, throwing gold around! You come home here with nothing! What are we supposed to live on? How about all your children? I'm not going to have this! I'm fed up!" Off she ran to the local magistrate who returned with her, threw Karna in chains and took him off to prison!

Next day, Karna, still in chains, was brought before the magistrate for trial. It was a formal occasion, the judge finely robed and bejewelled, and it fell first to the wife to tell the court what Karna had done. The magistrate was disturbed by her story, saying to Karna, "Oh, dear, oh dear! You had better explain yourself! What happened here? What mischief were you up to in that town?" So Karna explained to him. He said, "Well, as you see, my Lord, I'm a poor man and I've always been a poor man. According to the teaching of the Lord Buddha, if I don't give anything I will remain a poor man, not just in this life, but in many lives to come." And he continued explaining to the judge who, it should be said, was also a Buddhist. "I didn't really understand this until I arrived at the festival and suddenly it occurred to me that this is the reason why I'm a poor man: I never give anything! So I decided to give what I had to the Sangha with the idea of ensuring that in the future, at least, I will not be as poor as I am now."

The judge thought a bit, and finally said, "You're an honest man, Karna, and there's obviously no misdeed involved in what you've done. You've reduced your family to starvation in the process of doing it but I fully endorse what you've done. It is the teaching of the Lord Buddha, you're perfectly correct, so I can't do anything but impose on you the proper sentence, whatever that is, but," he went on, removing his beautiful collar of pearls, "I will give you my pearls – here you are – and my fine horse outside and that nice little village up the road, which will sustain you and your family for the rest of your lives."

This story is taken from *The Vinaya of the Mulasarvastivadins.*

# THE BURNING HOUSE

Once there was an Indian merchant who, though extremely rich and powerful, made his home in a crumbling old mansion, decayed almost to the point of collapse. Its windows were falling out, its floors riddled with dry rot and every other rot imaginable, its paint chipped and flaking, untouched for decades. But it was vast, this old heap, so vast that it couldn't be seen all at once, and it spread out without shape or design, its serpentine corridors twisting past countless shuttered rooms, winding up and down broken stairways and skirting doors that hadn't been opened for generations. Equally remarkable, this labyrinth possessed only two doors to the outside: a main entrance at the front and a little back door far away at the opposite end.

The wealthy man lived in his peculiar house with a family of many young sons and, presumably, many wives. They were all dispersed within the tumble-down building wherever they liked, settled in different corners and levels and landings according to their individual inclinations. Sometimes they were in touch with each other and sometimes they weren't. It was a house filled with people and yet, with each tucked away in his own private snuggery, it was filled with people who rarely met, and only two ways out!

The master went about his affairs in a manner usual for a busy merchant: one day at home and the next off for some important appointment. He was often away for many days at a time. Returning one evening from one of these long journeys, he was horrified to see plumes of smoke and tongues of flame flickering from the house, some close and some from far off parts. He realised instantly that very few of his children would even know that a fire had started, hived off as they were in their chosen nooks, and that once they learned of it they then had to find a way out through the maze of passageways, blocked rooms, blind corners, and quickly because their home was already a roaring inferno.

Tearing through the front door, he screamed and shouted for his children to run for their lives. "Fire, fire!" he shrieked. "Out of the house, now!" Perhaps in his panic his voice was unnaturally loud or his feet unnaturally fleet but somehow he managed to make all of them hear. They eventually gathered around him, coming from their different corners, some immediately on hearing his voice, others only after slowly finishing what they were doing, but each as if indulging an old chap whose imagination was playing up.

"Fire, father? Where? Can't see it, can't smell it. Are you sure you're not mistaken? After all, your sight's not what it used to be, you know!" and, "Well, Dad, perhaps you've had a tiring journey and you've imagined it. You see, none of us can see a sign of it, so well ... well, what's the panic, Dad?" But the father continued to plead with them. "You must come out of this house, you must! If you don't, you'll perish! And there are only two doors out for all of you, so hurry!" They listened respectfully, yet clearly they felt they knew better. Poor old Dad, really he is past it. Fancying the house is in flames! They smiled and nodded but they didn't budge.

The master knew that his children were very fond of playthings and toys. So he called out, "Right! I was only joking about the fire but in fact I've brought you some gorgeous presents!" "Presents? You've brought us presents from your trip? Oh, great! Why didn't you tell us that in the first place instead of wasting all that time on a story about a fire? Where are they? Who's got what?" "Ah, well," he said. "There's a special present for each and every one of you. I've chosen very carefully so that each of you gets exactly what he wants. I know each one of you very well and I know what each of you really wants and that's what I've picked out!"

"Where are they?" "Where are they?" "Outside! They're so big, I can't bring them in!" "So big, you can't bring them in?" "That's right! They're all waiting for you outside!" Straight out they ran, using both doors, and there in front of the burning house was a dazzling sight: no toys but full-sized chariots, one for each. All were embellished with parasols and each with a magnificent white horse in jewelled harness with plumes and feathers. They were splendid, and identical.

So the father got all of his children safely out of the burning house. How had he done it? By telling them a lie? Or the truth?

This story is taken from *The Lotus Sutra*.

# BODHISATTVA NEVER-DESPISE

This story is taken from *The Commentary on the Great Perfection of Wisdom*.

In ancient times, long before the life of our present Lord Buddha, there was another Buddha who lived and died in India and left behind his Dharma Teaching, as they all do. This Dharma went through the three stages of disintegration, as they all do, and though it had declined into the state called the counterfeit, it flourished still.

Living at this time was an elderly monk who was quite different from the other monks and nuns of the Order. He did not meditate or study sutras. He had his own rules. His practice was this: whenever he met anyone – monks, nuns or lay people – he would approach, bow low and say, "I respect you all, your reverences. I cannot hold any of you in contempt. You are all following the Path of the Bodhisattvas. You will all become Buddhas." He would bow again and go on his way.

At first no one objected. He was considered a little eccentric and he wasn't hindered in following his path but he was very persistent. Even if people were talking, he would interrupt in order to make his declaration. Some felt grossly insulted, others said, "Old man, you don't know what I'm doing! How do you know that I want to become a Buddha?" But none of these rebukes stopped the old monk. He continued to declare his belief to all, even if they wouldn't listen. He didn't elaborate, he just persisted. Nerves began to fray, tempers shortened, toleration turned to hostility. Pelted by sticks and stones, even by roof tiles, he was driven from the vicinity, all the while struggling to bow and offer respect.

Forced to wander the roads, still he followed his own path and continued his lonely practice. Finally, near the end of his life, he heard a Voice from the sky, a Voice which spoke directly to him and recited for him the whole of the Lotus Sutra. This old man, said by the Buddha to have been one of his own very early incarnations, was now fully awakened, with intuition confirmed, and has been known ever since as Bodhisattva Never-Despise.

# THE EXPLOITS AND PUNISHMENT OF THE ARHAT BHARADVAJA PINDOLA

The famous, and famously pious, Buddhist emperor Asoka reigned in India some two hundred years after the death of the Lord Buddha. It was Asoka's religious practice to make large gifts to the monks and nuns, especially those in his capital city Pataliputra, and on the great Buddhist festival days the lay people too gave food, clothing and medicine to their religious brethren in devout imitation of this good king.

On one such festival day, Pataliputra was crowded with people bringing these gifts and with monks and nuns drawn to the city from every corner of the realm. After all, Asoka's generosity was legendary: he usually gave enormous quantities of gold and silver! Indeed, so many came that only the most eminent waited within the main monastery where the emperor would pay his respects to Yasas, the chief abbot.

Asoka proceeded through the streets in solemn grandeur, accompanied by all the trappings of a state occasion. His subjects were thus instructed in his pious devotion to the Buddha's Dharma and encouraged to follow his example. He made his way to the monastery and into the central shrine, now filled with all the senior monks of the city. At the end of the shrine room was a raised dais bearing the great chair, the high throne of the chief abbot. As Asoka approached with reverent step, he saw the throne empty and Yasas standing to one side.

Suppressing his curiosity for the moment, the emperor bowed to the abbot, accepted his greetings and said all the expected things before finally asking, "Yasas, why are you standing today? Why is the high throne empty?" "Because," said Yasas, "one far more eminent than myself is coming here today to meet your majesty." Of course Asoka replied,

"I know of no one in this empire more eminent than yourself, Yasas. Of whom can you possibly be speaking?" "We are expecting the arrival of the great Arhat Pindola," said Yasas, "He was one of the thirty-six direct disciples of the Lord Buddha during his lifetime." Asoka thought about this for a minute. "But Yasas," he rejoined, "the Lord Buddha entered into Parinirvana over two hundred years ago! One of his direct disciples would have to be nearly three hundred years old!" "Exactly right, Sire. He is indeed nearly three hundred years old." "I've never heard the likes of it," cried the delighted emperor, "and he is coming here today?" "Expressly to meet your majesty." "Oh, that's good! How soon? When?" Yasas replied, "Any moment, Sire. Just look out toward the north. He'll soon appear."

They looked out. There in the distance but rapidly coming closer was a squadron of Arhats flying through the sky in their usual half-moon formation. Arriving over the monastery, they flew into the shrine room and landed on the dais, perfectly in place, cross-legged. All but one, that is. The ancient Pindola landed standing up. He walked to the high throne where he turned and sat down.

The great emperor, standing below this array of Arhats, made his prostrations to honour all the new arrivals, especially Pindola. He then looked carefully and saw that this three hundred year old person was tall and thin, with white hair streaming halfway down his back. His eyebrows, also white, were so long and straggly that they hung over his eyes, covering them completely. Asoka wondered if he could see at all. He raised his voice and welcomed Pindola to the empire with eloquent reverence. He then asked, "I have been told, venerable one, that you are the Arhat Pindola Bharadvaja who lived in the time of the Lord Buddha and attended him on many occasions."

Pindola was now standing, facing the emperor, but he couldn't see him until he lifted up his eyebrows. "Oh, there you are!" he exclaimed. "Yes, yes, that is so. I attended the Lord Buddha. Is there something you want to know?" The emperor was in fact desperate to know more about the Buddha. Everybody knew about his Dharma but even now, more than two hundred years after his death, no one knew what he had looked like or what sort of person he had been. There are no drawings of him, no images, no representations whatsoever. Asoka fervently desired to know about him personally: how he had looked and moved, what he had done and how he had done it. Here was the perfect person to tell him, someone who had actually attended the living Lord Buddha!

But first, he thought he'd clear up the other question that was now even more pressing. "Pindola," he asked, "how is it that you are three hundred years old? I mean, how come? Why don't you do like all the Arhats do and pass into Nirvana and make an end to Samsara?" Pindola sat comfortably, adjusted his eyebrows, and told Asoka this story.

When Pindola was a young man, not yet Arhat, he was very adept at magic. He loved the magical powers and he revelled in their exercise. He displayed his skill on any and every occasion. He also loved his food. Indeed, he was very greedy. Of course, as a monk, he could have only one meal a day and that was often a very meagre one. He found this part of the religious discipline extremely irksome as his tummy often started to rumble and he became very uncomfortable.

Well, one day, that is exactly what happened. He was going about his business, enjoying his magical powers. It was after midday and his stomach started up. Of course, there was another rule: no food after midday. "It's no good," he said to himself. "Never mind that I'm not supposed to eat again until tomorrow! I must get some food!"

It was Pindola's misfortune that just then the most sublime perfume wafted into his nostrils: cakes baking! The beautiful aroma wafted down the road from a little house where a woman was cooking for her family. "Yes, oh YES," decided Pindola, "those will do very nicely for me, right now!" So he followed his nose and it led him to the doorway of the kitchen. There he stood like a good monk, head down, bowl in hand, silently waiting. Even though there was saliva running down from the corner of his mouth, he remained composed. "Now behave yourself," he thought. He stood there and just waited but ... trouble!

As it happened, this particular housewife was fed up with Buddhist monks and their bowls, just standing and waiting. She was trying to feed her family, not his lot! It seemed to her that no sooner did she start to cook than a wretched monk appeared. Ignoring him did no good because the next day there'd be another and the next day there'd be three! So she snapped at Pindola, "Clear off! I don't want anything to do with you!" Not only could Pindola smell the cakes, he could see them and was close enough almost to touch them. He was leaning slightly their way and really salivating now but the deeply vexed housewife was adamant. "No!" she asserted. "I'm not giving anything to you or your kind! I'm tired of all of you!"

"I must have those cakes," Pindola said to himself. "Right! This calls for some magic." He remained at first in his still respectful silence, holding his bowl with humbly bowed head, the most innocent-looking monk, but all the pots and pans started dancing, dancing all around the kitchen! The housewife was shocked and tried to grab hold of this one and then that one as they skidded and scampered around the room but she didn't do very well. Meanwhile, Pindola was making all kinds of signs to her about the cakes. Monks are not allowed to ask for a gift so he did everything he could think of except to say, "I WANT A CAKE!"

The angry housewife ignored him, turning her back on him while snatching frantically at the dancing pots, so Pindola made things even harder for her. He turned the whole kitchen around so that when she tried to grab a pan to put it on the stove, it landed on one of her favourite chairs! She screamed and turned on him. "I know what you're doing, Pindola, it won't make any difference to me! You can do what you like but you are not getting my cakes!"

This challenge spurred him on. "All right," he thought, "if that's how you feel ..." And he then performed some of his most skilful tricks. He became many animals and ran around the room, frightening her nearly to death. He caused the kitchen to turn itself inside out. He lifted the whole house high in the air so that when the poor woman looked out of her door, she found herself a thousand feet above the ground! But even then, she would not give him a cake. Obviously, he had the skill to magic

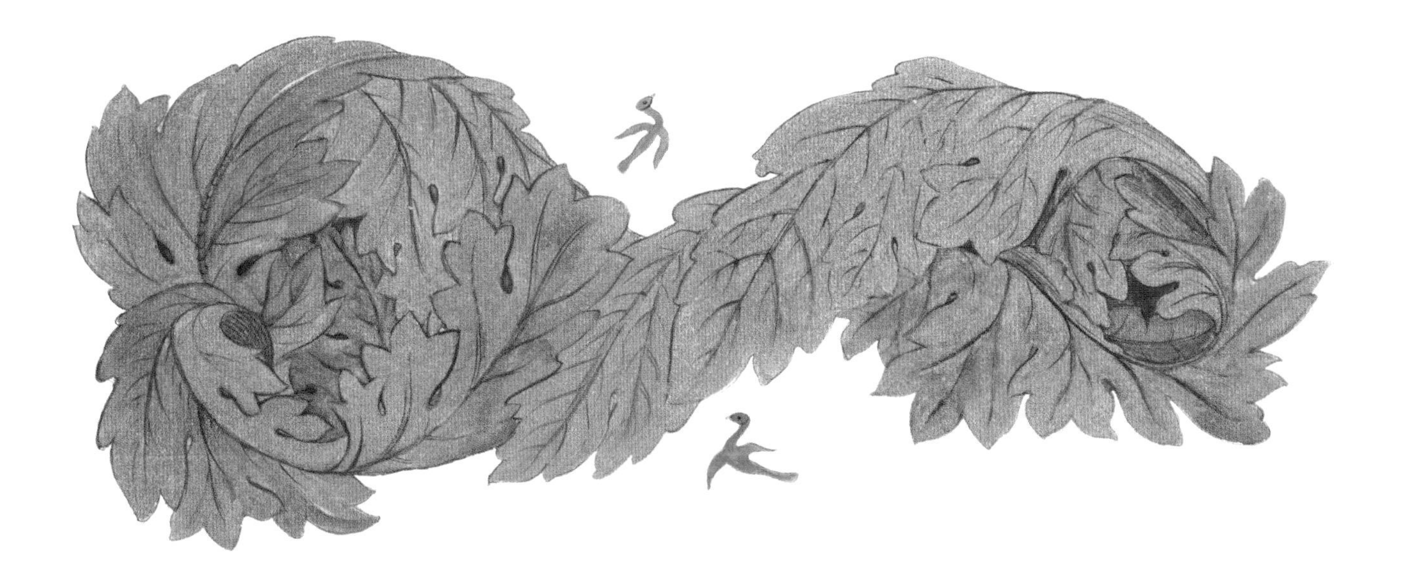

her cakes right into his bowl but the ban on asking for things, he reasoned, no doubt banned him from simply taking them, so he carried on, escalating his war of magic.

He whisked himself over to a nearby mountain and removed its top, just like a cone. He returned to the woman's house and lowered the mountain-top over the roof, declaring, "Right! Either I have my cakes or I drop it!" Not even the furious housewife could hold out against this kind of threat. She needed a roof over her head so at last she said, "Oh, blast you! There's your cakes!" and she flung him the whole panful.

The triumphant Pindola swallowed his cakes and gleefully danced round the town with the mountain-top. The townspeople were terrified! This mountain-top bobbing and rocking above them! What if it dropped? They would be killed! As their panic grew, one of them ran to the Lord Buddha and protested. "It's about time you controlled your people! Some joker-monk is playing around with a mountaintop over the town and he could kill us all!"

Pindola was calming down now, having enjoyed his cakes and his dance, and was replacing the mountaintop when his Master summoned him. "Pindola," asked the Buddha, "is it true that you ate cakes after time?" "Yes, Lord. I was hungry." "This is a fault, Pindola. And is it true that you threatened the housewife with all kinds of magical displays and that you danced around the town with the mountaintop?" "Yes, Lord." Now the Buddha became very serious. "You know that it is forbidden to display magical powers to lay people or, indeed, to anyone. Magical powers are not for vulgar display as you have used them. Not only have you terrified people with these powers, you have revelled in them. This is a grave fault and must be punished. Therefore, Pindola, you will not attain Nirvana, you will not die, you will live until the Dharma itself expires and whilst you live you will protect the Dharma in every way possible. I forbid you to attain Nirvana! You will stay here in Samsara for as long as the Dharma shall last!"

"And so," Pindola said to Asoka, "that is how I have come to wander the world, now nearly three

hundred years old, encouraging scholars and cheering up down-hearted monks. I must go on as long as the Teaching goes on. I shall not die until the Teaching dies. That is why I am here today."

Asoka spoke up. "Well now, Pindola, before you tell me any more of that I'd like to hear now about the Lord Buddha himself. I know you were with him when he punished you but you were also with him on many other occasions. I'd like you to tell me everything you can remember about how he looked and how he behaved. What sort of person was he? What did he do? How did he do it?" So Pindola said to Asoka, "Well, I was with the Lord Buddha when he performed the Miracle of the Fire and Water at Sravasti. I was with him, or rather I welcomed him, as he descended the heavenly stairway from the Heavens of the Thirty Three where he spent three months teaching the Abhidharma to his mother and the gods. I was with him at the Parinirvana when the earth shook and all beings were devastated. But," he continued, "I was with him on another occasion and that is the reason for my visit here today."

"It took place in this very kingdom, Asoka, long before you were its ruler. We were walking along a dusty road - well, actually, he was walking along this road and I was following close behind - and there, directly in the Buddha's path, were two little boys playing in the dust. Being directly behind him, I could see and hear everything. The little ones were playing at sand castles, or something like that, and the Buddha approached and stood there and, of course, they became aware of his presence, being only children. One of the boys looked up at the Buddha and picked up a handful of dust and placed it in the Buddha's bowl, as a gift, and the Buddha smiled."

"As you know, Sire," said the old Arhat to the emperor, "the Lord Buddha doesn't smile unless there is a very good reason. So I asked the Lord Buddha why he smiled and he said to me, "You see that boy there? He has just made a gift to me - worthless but he has made a gift - and because he gave and because of the thought that led to the gift and because of his good lineage, that young boy, some centuries after my death, will become a world-ruling emperor and his name will be Asoka. Now this is the reason I have come here today. Here you are, so anxious to know what the Buddha looked like and what he did and all the rest of it, but all the while you have seen the Buddha: you have given him a gift with your own hands in a previous life and you are now who you are because of it. You know the Buddha and the Buddha knows you."

The astonished and grateful Asoka thereafter became even more fervent in his devotion to the Dharma. He persuaded Pindola to take him to the very places where the Buddha was born, where he attained enlightenment, where he first preached and where he finally passed away and on these spots the great Asoka erected the famous iron pillars of north India, some of which are still standing to this day.

And also still standing, and sometimes sitting and sometimes flying but always wandering, it is said, through China and India and Central Asia is an old monk with long, long hair and long, long eyebrows, a monk who cannot die because he serves a Dharma that will last forever.

This story is taken from *The Exploits of Asoka*.

# THE BUDDHA RETURNS FROM A VISIT TO THE GODS

Now the reason for the Buddha's visit to the gods was to pay a call on his mother, who was residing in those realms as she had died soon after giving birth. She had no knowledge of his attainment of enlightenment and the teaching that followed. It seems to have been a requirement of a Buddha that he should visit his mother in the heavens and explain to her some of the topics from the Buddhist teachings.

After he had finished his various explanations of these topics to her, he let it be known to the Sangha of monks on Earth that he would soon be returning. We are not told exactly how he did this and neither are we told how his mother responded to the Buddhist teachings. If the present texts on Buddhist topics that we now have are anything to go by, these explanations would certainly have been very difficult to absorb at first hearing although, of course, when the Buddha himself is explaining these things the transmission is likely to be of another kind altogether. So while the Buddha was taking leave of his mother in the heavenly realms, on Earth vast crowds were assembling, led by all the monks and arhats of the Buddhist Sangha. They assembled at a place in North India called Sankasya. There, to this day, remains an iron pillar, which was erected by the great emperor Asoka several centuries after the event, to recall this incident.

As the crowds of people were gathering at Sankasya and the leading arhats of the Sangha were lining up to receive the Buddha after his journey, everyone was completely astonished to see, coming down from the sky, a grand stairway, which slowly descended until it almost, but not quite, touched the earth. This grand stairway was made of all the precious substances and the balustrades on either side were highly decorated and at certain marked-out intervals, all the way up into the sky, there were Buddhist symbols and images carved in ivory of such things as the great wheel and the trisula, the three-pronged sceptre, which is the symbol of the three jewels of the Buddha, Dharma and Sangha.

As soon as the stairway was fully extended, everyone looked up to see who would descend from it and shortly after three small beings appeared at the very top of the stairway, which, for the people on the ground, were almost indistinguishable as they were so far away. But gradually these three individuals slowly descended the grand stairway and, as they came nearer, everyone could see that the three personages were the Buddha, flanked on either side by the great gods Sakra and Brahma. Of course, these two great gods were dressed in the finest robes, wearing bracelets and necklaces and crowns on their heads and highly decorated coiffure whereas between them the Buddha Sakyamuni descended clad only in the simplest of robes, as was his normal attire.

When they reached the foot of the stairway they paused and they did not set foot on Earth at once. Straight away all the crowds of people, with the local royalty and all the arhats and monks and nuns of the Sangha, all prostrated in welcome and with shouts of joy. The leading arhat to welcome the Buddha back to Earth was Sariputra, who offered flowers and garlands to the two gods and words of praise to his master, the Buddha. Not all the arhats were in attendance at the foot of the grand stairway. One of the senior arhats, Subhuti, was in retreat in a cave nearby and although he was not there in the welcoming party he was fully aware of everything that was going on by the exercise of his supernatural powers. He was in two minds as to whether to attend the reception committee that was receiving the Buddha on his return or whether he should remain in his retreat and continue his deep meditation on Sunyata. After some consideration he decided he would remain where he was because he considered that this deep meditation on the Buddha's Dharma was the only proper reverence and respect that should be paid to the Buddha. So he stayed put.

At the very moment when the Buddha first set foot on Earth from the grand stairway, the two great gods disappeared. Presumably they went back to their own heavenly realms. Sariputra then addressed the Buddha and said how honoured he was to be the first to welcome the Buddha back from his heavenly journey. The Buddha replied, "Your welcome is not the first or the best that has been paid on this occasion. The first and the best welcome has been paid by the arhat Subhuti, who by entering the deep meditation on Sunyata is able to perceive the real Buddha and although he is not here in person yet, by doing what he does, he pays the most honour and respect to the Buddha on his return from the heavens." The Buddha continued, "You, Sariputra, and this whole assembly only pay homage to my worldly appearance but that is not the best homage and respect. All my appearances are mere illusory forms. Subhuti, by his deep meditations, has realised this and therefore he pays the best homage by perceiving the real body of the Buddha and that is the Dharmakaya."

Despite this mild reproof to Sariputra and the rest of the Sangha, who were in attendance at the foot of the stairway, there were great festivities and rejoicing in the town of Sankasya and its surroundings for some considerable time after this great descent. In the meantime, the Buddha and his monks quietly processed back to their monastery.

This story is taken from *The Commentary on the Great Perfection of Wisdom.*

# THE LEPER AND THE STATUE

There was a time, long ago, when Kashmir was profoundly Buddhist. Monasteries flourished, the teaching was widespread, the kings and their subjects were devout. A story is told from those days about a very pious Buddhist layman who suffered the devastation of contracting leprosy. In ancient times, in the East or in the West, a leper was an outcast: he had to be. This poor man knew that his life with family and friends was over. He had to leave them and find a cave, somewhere sheltered from the elements yet one near enough to a village so that he could beg for food.

He found such a cave and there he lived a miserable existence, which became more and more miserable as his disease worsened, but he had a particular devotion to the Bodhisattva Mahasattva Samantabhadra, whose name means 'Radiantly Gracious'. This Bodhisattva is always portrayed as shining, seated on a white elephant with six tusks, and arrayed in golden clothing or in some other way shown to be radiant. So, out of his fervent feeling for this Bodhisattva and because he had all the time in the world, he began to carve a statue of Samantabhadra on his elephant from the wall of his cave. This work went on for years and years, of course, and all the while the local people brought food to him and would leave it somewhere nearby. Finally the statue of the Bodhisattva on his elephant was finished, as large as life.

One evening, a townsman bringing food was astonished and rather alarmed to see light coming from the cave. He had not seen such a thing before so he approached cautiously until he could just see inside. There the leper was, prostrating himself before the statue and imploring the Bodhisattva to help him, to heal him. The townsman felt pity for him but thought, "Fat chance he's got of a cure, poor devil and that's only a statue he's made himself, anyway." But the light was intriguing, so he stayed and watched.

The prayers and prostrations went on for some time before the sick man sat back, quietly, in meditation. Then, the watching townsman froze in place. His hair stood on end! The Bodhisattva, radiating light, slowly leaned down from his elephant and reached out his stone hand. He stroked the limbs of the leper and they healed, then and there.

This story is taken from *The Commentary on the Great Perfection of Wisdom.*

# VIMALAKIRTI'S EMPTY HOUSE

In ancient India, in the great town of Vaishali, which, at the time of the Lord Buddha and after, was a separate and independent republic, there lived a very rich, very powerful, very well-known merchant layman called Vimalakirti. Now, in reality, Vimalakirti was not rich, nor powerful, nor a merchant. He was something quite different from that. He was a great bodhisattva who was masquerading as a rich and powerful merchant in Vaishali. Masquerading for a very special purpose, as will be seen.

To the Buddhist Order, however, he was just a white-robed layman and nothing more. The Lord Buddha and his Order of monks were in residence just outside Vaishali, in formal assembly, when they learned that the great merchant-layman of Vaishali was lying sick in his bed, unable to attend the assembly and hear the Buddha's discourse.

The Buddha, of course, in his usual compassionate manner, wanted to know who would go to visit Vimalakirti and enquire after his health and bring him flowers and a bunch of grapes or some such, as was the custom when visiting the sick. He turned first to Sariputra, at that time never far from the Buddha's side. "Why don't you, Sariputra, go and see the layman Vimalakirti and make the necessary enquiries? You can then come back and tell us." Sariputra said, "Oh, no, I'm not going to go to see Vimalakirti. Oh, no, I know what sort of a chap this Vimalakirti is. I met him before on the high road and he reduced me to complete silence. He is so eloquent and well-versed in the Dharma that I couldn't understand him and, well, I just couldn't say a thing. I'm too nervous to go and see Vimalakirti." So answered Sariputra.

The Buddha then queried all the arhats, right down the line of seniority, and each said something like, "Oh, no, Lord, please don't ask me to go. Ask me anything else, Lord, but not to talk to Vimalakirti. He's too advanced for me. I just can't make head nor tail of him. He's a real slippery customer and I want nothing to do with him. I don't care if he's sick. I am not going." Unprecedented! The Buddha asking his Arhats to go and do something and they refuse! So he turned to his bodhisattvas, rank upon rank of them. "How about you, Bodhisattva so-and-so? Will you go and visit Vimalakirti?" Same thing. "Oh, no!" came the reply. "Just like the arhats, I am having nothing to do with him. He's too far beyond anything I can cope with. If I asked him how he was feeling, he'd probably do something awful."

Now the arhats and the bodhisattvas didn't just refuse flatly. They were adamant! "No way am I going to see him!" But each did offer an explanation. In every case it was an encounter with Vimalakirti in which the layman had overturned or discomfited the monk, had shown him to be in some way lacking in perfect wisdom. So, having gone all round his Order, the Buddha's final hope was the great bodhisattva Manjusri.

"Well, Manjusri, you're not going to let me down, are you? Someone should go and enquire about Vimalakirti's health. It is not fitting that we should just sit here and say he's too severe for us. Someone has got to go. How about you?" Manjusri said, "If you insist, Lord, but I don't want to go." The Buddha, finding at last a half-willing victim, said, "Yes, I insist. Go!"

Now, while all this was going on, the "sick" Vimalakirti was lying on his bed in his house in Vaishali. The townspeople there heard of his condition and trooped to his door in great numbers, bringing little gifts and good wishes. And he, being quite other than what he seemed, could lie there receiving them while at the same time listening in to the Order's discussion through his supernatural powers.

He was probably having a good laugh at this arhat and that bodhisattva as each described yet another humiliation at his hands when he realised that his visitor was to be Manjusri. "Right," he said to himself. "For Manjusri, we must arrange a special welcome!" And he set about the task of preparing his house to receive the Bodhisattva of Wisdom. A task of magic, of course.

When the Order heard Manjusri agree to the visit, they were abuzz and decided to go along and watch. "These two characters will have quite a time together! Can't miss this!" So they all deserted the Buddha (he stayed in place) and headed off with Manjusri for Vimalakirti's house: a huge crowd of arhats, bodhisattvas, monks, nuns and lay people surging along the road to enjoy the fun. Sariputra was there and all the rest.

Manjusri, in the lead, entered the house and looked around. Very strange! "What's going on here?" he asked himself for in the reception room was nothing but Vimalakirti's couch, with the layman stretched upon it in white robes. No chairs, tables, mats, hangings, lamps, flowers, no family or servants or retainers in sight. The entire house was absolutely, totally, empty of everything except the bed, and that in the centre of the room, with himself lying upon it. Nothing else, all empty, completely deserted.

Despite his curiosity at this startling sight, Manjusri approached Vimalakirti and entered first upon the formalities. "How are you feeling?" he asked and, "Have you had the sickness long? Are the pains severe? Are you taking the proper medicine?" and so forth. To these enquiries Vimalakirti gave the stock answers as visits to the sick in those days were conducted according to strict etiquette. Even a dying man would have replied, "I'm feeling fine, thank you."

The conventions honoured, no doubt including even the bunch of grapes, Manjusri went on. Vimalakirti had earlier replied that the illness had lasted for some considerable time, so Manjusri now asked, "How is it you have been sick so long? Why is that?" Vimalakirti's response was to this effect: "I am ill because all beings are ill and as long as all beings are ill I remain ill." Manjusri also asked, "And why is your house empty? Where are all your servants and where is your wife and family? Where is all your furniture? Why are you lying ill in an empty house?" Vimalakirti answered something like, "The whole world and all beings are empty. And that is why my house is empty. As long as all beings and the world is empty my house will remain empty." There followed a subtle and complicated exchange of Dharma talk about these ideas. It was on a very high level indeed, carried on not for each other's benefit but for the benefit of all those in the room. It wasn't easy to follow but not everyone in the room was trying.

Sariputra suddenly became aware that he and all the other arhats and bodhisattvas and the monks and the nuns and all the lay people and townspeople of Vaishali were contained in this one room. A perfectly ordinary room, yet half the population of the republic was in it! Scores of arhats, hundreds of bodhisattvas and Vimalakirti on his couch, all in one room, nobody squeezed or crushed or crowded together. Extraordinary! And he thought, "Where are all these great beings going to sit?" (Not for him the intricacies of the Dharma-talk. No! Quite down-to-earth was Sariputra, much more interested in questions of comfort.) Vimalakirti knew this. He read Sariputra's thoughts and said to him, "Have you come here concerned with the Dharma, Sariputra, or have you come here concerned with where you are going to sit?"

"Nasty," thought Sariputra, "that's exactly why people are afraid of him." Aloud he replied, "Who, me? Oh, no no. I mean, yes. Well. Oh, well. Just carry on, Vimalakirti." But Vimalakirti replied, "That being your thought, I will shortly show you such seats as you have never seen before and," he continued, "if you think this room is crowded now, well, there are about a hundred thousand very large bodhisattvas on their way to join us. Where are you going to seat them?" Sariputra was silent, quite speechless. "They're coming to watch us and hear what we're doing," Vimalakirti continued, "and they're very big!"

In an instant, Vimalakirti created hundreds of high thrones, huge ones, sized to hold the giant bodhisattvas about to arrive. They soon appeared. Paying their respects, they said that they came from their Buddha in another universe and that they came to hear the teaching being given by Vimalakirti with Manjusri. Vimalakirti said from his couch, "You are welcome! Please take a seat," and turning to Sariputra said, "Please show our guests to their seats." Sariputra obeyed and the hundred thousand enormous bodhisattvas sat on the hundred thousand huge thrones and they and everyone who had come before them was perfectly comfortable. Still no crush. Still an empty room!

Watching and listening to all this was a goddess, a devi, who, because she was a devi, was invisible but she was very much there nonetheless and, in fact, had been an attendant on Vimalakirti for many years. And when all the great bodhisattvas had arrived and she heard the dialogue between Manjusri and Vimalakirti, she decided to become visible in human form. She appeared as a woman in all the regalia of a goddess: headdress, long silk garments, jewels, bangles, ropes and ropes of pearls: all the accoutrements of a female Indian deity. She manifested while scattering flower petals on the arhats and bodhisattvas. This was a sign of respect often employed by gods and goddesses. When the Buddha was preaching, for example, they might well appear, sprinkling petals all over just to keep the dust down, so to speak. She did this to the whole assembly.

The petals that touched the bodies of the bodhisattvas merely brushed over them and fell off on to the ground. Petals that touched the bodies of the arhats, however, stuck. Petals were sticking all over their bodies and they tried to flick them off. They couldn't do it! They were stuck tight! Sariputra was very annoyed.

The devi came up to him and asked, "Venerable Sir, why are you trying to remove the flowers? What's wrong with them?" Sariputra said, "It is not fitting. It is not proper. It is not allowed that monks of the Lord Buddha's Order be adorned with flowers. We are monks and we are governed by rules. They must come off! I can't have these flowers all over me. It is humiliating!" The devi then said, "Observe, Sariputra, the flowers don't stick to the bodies of the bodhisattvas." "Oh," he said, "that is their affair. They can look after themselves. I can't get them off me!" The devi asked, "Do you realise why the flowers can't be brushed off, why they stick to you?" "No," answered Sariputra. "Well," she told him, "it is because you constantly distinguish between what is proper and what is not proper and what is fitting and what is not fitting and you cleave to this and reject that and you grasp at one set of false views after another." This to an Arhat! "And because of the grasping and rejecting nature of your mind, the flowers will not leave your body. They will stick to you like all your false views stick to you." So poor Sariputra was humiliated again!

The devi then, with the magical powers of a goddess, removed the flowers from all the arhats and, as one, they sighed deeply in relief. "Thank goodness that's over!"

Sariputra studied this person, the devi, shamefacedly wondering how a mere woman could know so much. He asked, "Do you come here often?" "Well," she replied, "as a matter of fact I've been coming here for some years listening to the Dharma preached by Vimalakirti." "How do you know so much?" he demanded to know. "How do you know this flower trick? After all, you're only a woman. I'm an arhat!" Anyone but Sariputra could have seen he was going to be bounced hard!

She asked, "How do you know I'm a woman?" He replied confidently, "I can see what's in front of me, can't I? Of course you're a woman!" The devi abruptly used her magic powers again and transformed Sariputra into her body and herself into his but with each remaining his and her self on the inside. Sariputra suddenly looked down. "What's all this?" he stammered in astonishment. "Where's all this come from?" And he looked up to see, himself. And the voice of the female goddess spoke to him from the body which was in every outward detail Sariputra's. "Now, Sariputra, are you still sure that I am a woman and are you sure of what you are? Look!"

Of course he saw that he was dressed in the tiara and the beads and the bangles and all the rest of it. He was completely nonplussed. "What are you doing to me?" he protested. "How has this happened?" The devi then explained to him, at some length actually, that the Lord Buddha has said that the dharmas, the real elements of existence, are neither male nor female. "The bodies we inhabit are illusory. There is no distinction in essence or in fact or in reality between men and women. They are merely appearances and nothing more." "Yes, yes," agreed Sariputra readily. "You are quite right, I am wrong, but let me have my body back!" She obliged and turned them round again. They were back in their old selves. Poor Sariputra! Humbled a third time and totally at a loss!

So Vimalakirti himself intervened and explained. "In a way, Sariputra, you have been misled. This being is neither a woman nor a goddess. She is a great bodhisattva who comes whenever the Buddha's deep Dharma is being preached. She has attended on innumerable Buddhas of the past. She is in fact a non-reverting bodhisattva who can display any form she wishes!" And all the assembly praised the wisdom and skilful means of both the goddess and Vimalakirti.

This story is taken from *The Teaching of Vimalakirti.*

# THE BOWL OF PERFUMED FOOD

The scene is as before. A person in white robes is lying on a couch in the centre of a completely empty room. There is no chair, no table, not a stick of furniture. There is absolutely nothing in the room but the man on the couch. This man is Vimalakirti and he is masquerading as a layman, although he is nothing of the sort, and he is masquerading as ill, too ill to attend the Buddha's interminable meeting going on right now outside town. Arriving in the room are many of the monks from the Buddha's Order, among them a great number of arhats and high-ranking bodhisattvas, and gathering outside is a large throng of lay people and townsfolk coming to ask about Vimalakirti's health and see that he has everything he needs.

Leading the delegation from the Order is Manjusri, the bodhisattva of wisdom. He sees the empty room and, in it, a teaching opportunity so, for the benefit of their presumably enraptured listeners, Manjusri and Vimalakirti enter into a dialogue expounding the Doctrine of The Empty House. But they're not enraptured at all. They may look quiet and attentive but actually they're bored and hungry. They don't understand a word. Anxiously, Sariputra sneaks a look at the sun. "When are we going to eat?" he thinks. "We can't eat after midday and it's nearly that now. These two jokers going on and on ... if they don't stop soon, we won't eat at all!"

Vimalakirti has a very nasty and disturbing habit of reading people's thoughts. At this very moment he tunes in to Sariputra's. Breaking off the dialogue with Manjusri, he calls out, "Sariputra, have you come here for the food or for the teaching?" Sariputra nervously straightens his robes. "Oh, for the teaching, of course!" Vimalakirti states, "No, you're waiting for food so I will now see that you get such food as you have never tasted before." No longer bored, the assembly really pays attention. "What's going to happen now?" everybody wonders.

Vimalakirti announces, "In the far recesses of the universe is a Buddha-field called the Sarvasughanda, this means the 'Perfumed Land', and the Buddha of that universe is now living there and teaching his Order. I would like to send a message from here to there and ask him for a portion of the midday meal which he and his assembly are about to eat. Who will go?"

Silence, no volunteers. Manjusri has exercised one of his powers, the ability to make people speechless. No one can speak up even if they want to. Manjusri wants Vimalakirti to have free rein for what he's about to do so he's not surprised when no one offers to go. "Aren't you all ashamed of yourselves?" says Vimalakirti. "You great leaders, you bodhisattvas, and you in particular, Manjusri, not one of you will do this simple thing for me: just going from here to the end of the universe with a message! I am ashamed of you all."

"You shouldn't look with contempt upon the Buddha's followers," chides Manjusri gently. Vimalakirti snorts, "I'll do it myself!" and with his magical powers he constructs, in front of them all, a mind-made bodhisattva, complete with head-dress, robes and ornaments. To this being Vimalakirti says, "I want you to go to the Buddha of Sarvasughanda and present him with the compliments of Vimalakirti of the Saha Universe. Tell him that Vimalakirti is preaching here the universal Dharma, just as he is doing there, but that in order to continue, Vimalakirti needs to borrow the remains of the Buddha's bowl of food after he has finished his midday meal."

The mind-made bodhisattva bows to Vimalakirti and vanishes from the house. In a flash he has travelled the immeasurable distance to the Universe of the Perfumed Garden. There, everyone and everything is made of perfume. The Dharma consists of perfume. The Order, all bodhisattvas, are all made of perfume. The Dharma is dispensed by perfume. The messenger from the Saha Universe pays his respects and delivers Vimalakirti's message asking for food. The perfume bodhisattvas stare at him, he is so unlike them. They have never seen anyone like him: so solid and with such a nasty smell.

Their Buddha remonstrates with them, "You mustn't look down on this creature from Saha," he tells them, as if they could stop themselves. "I remember Vimalakirti," he goes on. "Well, is that where he's gone? Couldn't be in a worse spot, poor devil. If he wants the remains of my bowl of food then by all means he must have it," and he hands over a bowl of perfumed rice to the mind-made bodhisattva, who prepares to leave.

The perfume bodhisattvas become very curious about the Saha Universe. "Where is it?" they ask. "Who is Vimalakirti?" Their Buddha explains that Vimalakirti is a great bodhisattva in another universe and that he is helping Sakyamuni teach the Dharma in one of the lowest world systems in that universe. "The creatures there are very hard and preaching to them is one tough job," he says. "May we go with the Saha creature back to that universe and have a look?" they ask. "Only if you make your bodies different from what they are now," the Buddha replies. "To go there in the glorious bodies you have here will provoke envy in the Saha universe and make things even worse for them, and it's bad enough. So make yourselves bodies fitted for the occasion and the place."

Now all of this takes only a few minutes of earthly time and off they go with the mind-made bodhisattva and the bowl of perfumed rice. They crowd into Vimalakirti's empty house and as the food is distributed its perfume spreads all about, into the town, everywhere. The wonderful scent pervades everything and it is so strong that people are drawn from every corner to find out where it's coming from. The entire population of the town arrives at Vimalakirti's house, thousands of people, and all he has is this one bowl of rice.

Everybody, not only the monks, sees this one bowl, and they worry. "That's not going to go very far," they think. Sariputra looks at his watch again and again. "It's very close to midday," he frets. "If the monks aren't fed soon it will be too late. What a rough day this is going to be: very little food, if any!"

Once again Vimalakirti reads their minds. "You should not have ill-natured or disrespectful thoughts about the food donated by the Buddha of the Perfumed Garden," he tells them. "If all the beings of the world were to feed from this bowl for years on end they would not diminish it by one iota. If you have such thoughts you will not be able to digest this food and it will make you ill. If you accept this food with respect you will be able to progress even more rapidly with your Dharma practice and comprehension."

Many of the monks are sceptical but the bowl passes round and everyone eats. They all eat well and the food doesn't diminish at all. And as it passes through their bodies, the perfume permeates every pore so that every one give off the perfume of the Dharma and each, whether bodhisattva or leper, advances one full stage on his chosen Path. All are satisfied and wonder-struck.

This story is taken from *The Teaching of Vimalakirti*.

# THE INEXHAUSTIBLE LAMP

In the market place in the city of Vaishali, a Buddhist monk was making his rounds through the city, begging for his food as they used to do in ancient times. The monk arrived in the marketplace and was there accosted by a merchant who told him that he was so impressed by his demeanour that he would like to give him a special gift.

It has to be said at once that this merchant was no merchant at all. He was Mara, the god of all the passions and all the lies and deceits that occur in this world. In the same way that Vimalakirti would attempt to establish the true Dharma and to protect its practitioners, Mara would adopt any guise in order to do the opposite.

Mara proposed to the monk that he accept a gift: his retinue of women, who were attending on their master. Of course, the monk was horrified at any such proposal and he protested loudly that monks are not allowed to accept such gifts. In most cases they are not allowed to have any commerce with women whatsoever. At that point, Vimalakirti appeared on the scene and approached the monk and Mara and said, "I know exactly who you are and what your intention is and you should be ashamed of yourself for trying to tempt this poor monk with the present that you know very well he cannot accept."

Now Mara in his turn, for after all he is a god, knew who was speaking to him: the great bodhisattva Vimalakirti. Mara was afraid of his power. Vimalakirti continued speaking, "As you see, I am a layman and there would be nothing wrong in offering to me these women that you have in train. It is a gift which I will accept quite readily." Realising that his attempt to entangle the monk in wrong-doing had failed because of Vimalakirti's intervention, Mara tried to vanish away but Vimalakirti's power held him rooted to the spot. "Well, Mara, are you going to give me these women or not?"

Mara, completely terrified by what Vimalakirti might do, agreed to hand over his retinue of women and, after doing so, quickly hid himself away. Vimalakirti, in a respectful manner, sent the bemused monk on his way. After that he gathered the women around him as their new master and expounded to them in detail the benefits of the 'garden of the Dharma'. It has to be understood that all the women from Mara's retinue were all experts in the arts of love. In fact that is all they did know. In listening to this man expounding the pleasures of the garden, the women were completely enthralled and wished to know more. By means of his special powers, Vimalakirti then encouraged and persuaded them to raise the thought of enlightenment. Because of their respect for and interest in their new master, all the women did so, under his instruction.

Now Mara, who had been watching these events from a distance, demanded to have his entire retinue of women back. All the women protested at Mara's intervention and said, "We do not wish to go back with you. You have given us to this man and he has promised us the pleasures of the 'garden of the Dharma' which we all wish to see and enjoy." But Vimalakirti said to them, "You should go back and serve your original master, Mara, because I'm afraid my own household is quite full and because of that I would not be able to take you with me."

On hearing this, Mara's women became very dejected. Vimalakirti explained to them that because they had raised the thought of enlightenment, their situation had completely changed. He reminded them that in that situation – having raised the thought of enlightenment, that is the wish and aspiration to gain full enlightenment and thereby enjoy the pleasures and benefits of 'the garden of the Dharma' – they were no longer the same women that they were before and, in that case, whether they were in one place or another, residing with Mara or with him, made no difference to how things stood. He then told them to return with their original master and that he would give them a parting gift called 'The Short Treatise on the Inexhaustible Lamp'.

The lamp that Vimalakirti referred to is the ancient kind of lamp with a bowl containing flammable oil and a wick which soaks up the oil and, when lit, burns until the oil has been completely consumed.

Vimalakirti then said, "A single lamp can light thousands of other lamps without itself being dimmed in the slightest. Those who have been illumined by the Great Way can help to illuminate others wherever they might be and without reducing their own inner light in the slightest degree." The retinue of women went off with their master but with knowing smiles.

This story is taken from *The Teaching of Vimalakirti.*

# THE MAGICAL CONTEST BETWEEN SARIPUTRA AND MAUDGALYAYANA

Seated atop Vulture Peak, Sariputra was mending his waistband. He had been just about to leave for an important gathering of the Buddha and all his arhats, a meeting on a faraway lake high in the Himalayas, when he noticed that the edges of his belt were frayed. Very bad form, he thought, to arrive there tattered: better to be a trace late, surely, but dressed respectfully.

At that very same moment on the lofty distant lake on Mount Meru, the World Mountain, lotus blossoms were opening. The Buddha and his arhats were arriving by air, flying from faraway places in perfect lotus position, and now descending gracefully, each landing in balance on a welcoming flower. The blossoms formed a great circle. At its centre, the most beautiful lotus of all received the Lord Buddha himself.

"Ah," said he, looking around, "We are not yet all here: Sariputra is missing. Maudgalyayana rose instantly from the fragrant flower onto which he had just settled and in a span of time too brief to measure flew across the thousand miles to Sariputra. The Buddha turned to his comrades and said, "Maudgalyayana may have a little problem to solve when he gets there. He and Sariputra have always been rivals, playing tricks and setting traps, one for the other, even in past lives." And he told this story:

"There was once a master painter who went travelling, looking for work. His quest took him to that part of the country ruled by the Greeks, called Bactria. There he visited the household of an equally masterly artisan who offered him work and invited him to stay for a while. His host showed him to his bedroom. Shortly thereafter, a most beautiful serving maiden arrived. Silently, the young woman performed her tasks: gently washing his feet and then giving him delicious food and drink. When he finished eating, she stayed, gazing at him without speaking. 'Ah,' thought the happy painter, 'she obviously fancies me and I do find her most attractive.' So he moved to her side and put his arm around her. Taking her hand in his, he began to kiss each exquisitely shaped finger. Her hand fell off! He recoiled violently, causing the arm to follow. Her other arm then thudded to the floor, the head rolled, the legs crashed down, the torso bounced away. A trick! A mechanical doll so perfect that the trained eye of a master painter thought it living!

"He would now be a laughing stock, of course, his reputation ruined. A painter deceived by a puppet. But at least, he realised, this grievous humiliation had taken place in private. Perhaps a public revenge would save him. So he took his colours and brushes into a corner of the room, under an arch, and spent the night painting.

"He was not seen the next morning, nor yet at midday, so the puzzled artisan tapped at the bedroom door. No answer. He pushed it open carefully and peered in. To his horror, he saw beyond the scattered pieces of his mechanical doll the body of his guest, hanging by the neck from the arch, his paints and brushes in great disorder at his dangling feet. The appalled artisan was crushed with guilt. He had intended only a good joke, never this. Obviously the shocked painter had felt himself such a failure that he could not go on. The artisan ran for the authorities since by Greek law the king had to be told of any unusual death.

"The King's officers came. They saw the horrifying scene – a woman's body in pieces and a man's hanging by the neck – and listened to the explanations and self-recriminations of the remorseful artisan. "Ah, yes," they agreed, "a great tragedy. We accept that it was an accident, however, and we will now remove the body and take it away." They took their swords and went to the arch to cut the rope. A painting! No rope, no neck, no body, just paint so cleverly applied that not one of them had doubted its truth! The jubilant painter leapt out of the corner in which he had hidden and enjoyed his public triumph.

"He was, of course, Sariputra in a previous life and the artisan was Maudgalyayana. So we must wait," concluded the Buddha and he and the arhats settled down on their blossoms on the high windy lake.

Maudgalyayana found Sariputra head down, working laboriously at the ragged edge of his waistband. "Sariputra," he scolded, "how can you keep the Lord Buddha waiting while you sew? Have you forgotten that the arhats are to gather to expound their past lives? Come along now!" Sariputra responded calmly that he must finish his task: he would be ashamed to appear before the Lord Buddha in a tatty old waistband. "Nonsense," snapped Maudgalyayana, "and anyway you don't seem able to sew very well. Give it here and let me show you how." Sariputra complied. Maudgalyayana took the belt and, instantly transforming his ten fingers into ten steel needles, repaired the worn fabric with the speed of flashing light.

"Oh, wonderful," cooed Sariputra. "Now that is a really fine trick, Maudgalyayana, and so useful, too. Could you teach me that?" "Oh, stop wasting time, Sariputra. Put on your belt and let's go!" "Well, I'd be happy to, if you'll just pick it up for me." Sariputra had placed it on the ground. Maudgalyayana snatched at it in exasperation but it would not move. He pulled it harder. It would not move. Sariputra's magic had attached it to Vulture Peak. So Maudgalyayana exerted his own magic powers and pulled so hard that the entire mountain began to shake and tremble.

Sariputra felt the Peak moving under him. "This man may do it," he thought, so he magically re-attached the belt to Mount Meru, the World Mountain. "Try again, Maudgalyayana," he urged. Again, the waistband stuck fast, so Maudgalyayana doubled his strength. He pulled so hard that the World Mountain began to move, and with it the waters of the lake upon which the Buddha and his arhats waited, composed upon gently bobbing lotus blossoms. But now the bobbing became swaying and the swaying became tumbling, as the lake waters churned from the unseen force. Composure lost, the arhats clung frantically to petals and tendrils. "Help, help," came the cries, "we're drowning. Save us, oh Lord, we're falling!"

Sariputra, too, feared that Maudgalyayana would destroy the whole world with his power so he quickly transferred the belt's magical connection from the World Mountain to the very lotus upon which the Buddha sat, bonding it to its deep core. "Try one more time, Maudgalyayana," he cried. But as soon as Maudgalyayana gripped the waistband, he knew where it led and he opened his hands. He might be able to move mountains but not even his magic could move the Buddha.

"All right, Sariputra, you win. Let's go!" "Right, Maudgalyayana, but I'm already there!" Sariputra had vanished. Maudgalyayana followed and found him settled upon a lotus within a circle of serene arhats bobbing gently up and down around the central blossom of the Buddha. Maudgalyayana made a perfect landing on the last empty flower on the shimmering lake.

"Now," said the Lord Buddha, "we will tell about our past lives."

This story is taken from *The Vinaya of the Mulasarvastivadins.*

# THE PIGEON AND SARIPUTRA'S SHADOW

It is known that the Lord Buddha was usually accompanied on his walks and travels by his disciple, Ananda, but there was an occasion when, instead of Ananda, it was Sariputra who went along with him on a walking exercise. The Buddha, of course, walked in front and Sariputra behind and as they walked along, out of the sky came a pigeon that was being chased to his death by a hawk. The pigeon made a sudden dive to escape the hawk and alighted in their path, just a few paces ahead of the Buddha. The Buddha's shadow, as he approached, fell across the trembling bird, lying there expecting that its last moment had come. As the shadow covered it, the pigeon stopped trembling. He became calm and started to coo. He sat still and peaceful.

Now behind the Buddha came the walking Sariputra. He saw that the Buddha had stopped, so he came up beside him to see why. As he came round his master's side, Sariputra's shadow fell across the tranquil bird and immediately it became agitated again, trembling and crying.

Sariputra, if the truth be told, was more than a little annoyed by this. He said, "Well, why, Lord, when your shadow fell across the pigeon, he was calm and content but when my shadow falls across the pigeon, he gets all agitated again? I mean, you and I are both arhats: we have both destroyed all the passions. The pigeon has nothing to fear from either you or me so why does the pigeon tremble when my shadow crosses it? It's not fair!"

The Buddha turned to him and said, "This, Sariputra, is because the traces of defilements have not been fully extirpated in you. Only the Buddha fully extirpates all the traces, not only the active passions but the traces: the roots and seeds of the defilements. That is why, when your shadow crossed the pigeon, he became alarmed. He doesn't know you are an arhat. He doesn't know your name is Sariputra." The Buddha continued, "Sariputra, why not exercise your great powers of concentration and cast your mind back along all the previous existences of this pigeon and see if you can discover why he is still a pigeon."

It is a practice of the superpowers by those who have reached the advanced level of the path to observe and know directly all their own past lives and, in certain cases, all the future lives of certain individuals. So, at the Buddha's request, Sariputra entered into the special concentration required for this feat and observed and considered all the pigeon's past lives. He went back through eighty thousand kalpas of that pigeon's line of previous existences and the pigeon remained a pigeon. He had never been anything else but a pigeon.

Sariputra came out of his concentration and said to the Buddha, "I have done this. I have gone back eighty thousand kalpas and I can't go back beyond that and in any case it makes no difference because the pigeon remains a pigeon all the time. It is not going to make any difference." "You may be right, Sariputra, you may be right," said the Buddha. "but," he continued, "the important thing is, what is going to happen to the pigeon in future, isn't it, so now cast your mind forward, Sariputra, in the case of this pigeon, and tell me what his future is to be."

Sariputra then entered into the appropriate concentration and considered the future retribution, the fruition of the pigeon's future existences. He looked forward a further eighty thousand kalpas and the pigeon remained a pigeon. Sariputra gave up in disgust. "This is a waste of my time. I mean, this pigeon is a pigeon! Why are we concerned about this pigeon?" And he told the Buddha that he could see no improvement or worsening of the pigeon's state. He would remain a pigeon for innumerable existences, up to eighty thousand kalpas anyway.

"How far ahead did you look, Sariputra?" "Eighty thousand kalpas, Lord. Isn't that far enough?" "Not really."

The Buddha looked at the pigeon and said to Sariputra, "You are quite correct, Sariputra. This pigeon will remain a pigeon for eighty thousand kalpas but there will come a time after that when the pigeon will gain human birth and he will gain human birth in the lifetime of the Buddha so-and-so," whom he named, "in the era of the so-and-so," which he named. "This pigeon, after becoming human, will then take refuge in that Buddha and his Dharma and become a layman. After that Buddha has passed into Parinirvana, the layman will also pass away and be reborn many times, always in a human birth, and eventually he will be reborn in the time of yet another Buddha," whom he named, "in the era of the so-and-so," which he named. "Under that Buddha, that layman will first raise the thought of enlightenment and then he will enter the Bodhisattva Path. He will practise the Bodhisattva Path for immeasurable kalpas and finally that layman, who will have descended from this pigeon here, will eventually himself become the Buddha So-and-So," and the Lord Buddha named him, all his titles, and the era and he said to Sariputra, "Eighty thousand kalpas is not enough, Sariputra, but I am not surprised because really only Buddhas can see that far ahead, not arhats."

This story is taken from *The Commentary on the Great Perfection of Wisdom*.

# THE ARHATS' AIRLIFT

The events now to be related took place in ancient India, well before the time of the great emperor Asoka, in the ancient capital of one of the kingdoms of northern India called Pataliputra. This great city was built on the banks of the lower Ganges and is now called Patna. There was a large Buddhist community in this city and all over Northern India because the Buddha had appeared, delivered his teaching and then died in the area at least a century before these events took place.

Although the king, who resided in this city, was not himself a Buddhist he was certainly very tolerant of his subjects who were. Of course, with a large Buddhist community there were several Buddhist monasteries in the capital and already there were divergences in the interpretation of the Buddhist doctrine being held in different quarters of the monastic community. One of these differences became so deep and intransigent that the dispute caused a fracture in one of the monasteries, so much so that the monks in this great monastery would not celebrate their general confession together.

As was often the case in these ancient times among the Indian Buddhists, the laity took a keen and informed interest in what went on within the monastery and, of course, from time to time laymen and laywomen would attend the monastery and listen to lectures and homilies by the monks. This meant that the laity of the capital became well aware of the fracture of relations within the great monastery and they were scandalized at the behaviour of the monks who would not perform their required rituals together.

This dispute, which we won't bother to give in any detail, was no small matter. However, it concerned one of the basic doctrines that the Buddha himself had promulgated during his lifetime. In fact it concerned the primary matter of the elements of existence, the dharmas, and whether these dharmas only existed momentarily in the present or whether in fact they existed in some form in the future to allow them to come to birth in the present.

Now all this would be rather obscure to the average layman but the fact of the matter was that the difference of opinion was so hotly contended on each side that it spread throughout all the other monasteries of the capital. It seemed that nothing could reconcile the two parties and the regular life of all the monasteries became completely disrupted. This disruption went on for a considerable time, in such a way that the laity became disgusted with the attitude and behaviour of all the monks and their dispute began to spread among the lay people of the capital as well. Needless to say the lay people knew little or nothing about the particulars of the dispute but they also became divided over what should be done about it.

Very shortly there were disturbances in the streets and angry protests at the monasteries and gradually this general behaviour descended into unrestrained rioting. At this point some of the leading officials of the capital became alarmed at the breakdown in order and they petitioned the king to send in the army to quell the riots and restore order. This the king did and once order was restored in the only way that kings know how, that is to say by brute force, the whole city was then confronted with the problem of how to resolve this dispute amongst the monks in the monasteries. It was decided, in view of the seriousness of the previous situation, to call in several of the leading monks on both sides of the dispute and have them put their case for and against in front of the king, who would arbitrate as to what should be done. And so there was a debate between the two parties in the king's presence.

Of course it can easily be imagined that the king of this time, or any other time come to that, would know little or nothing about what they were talking about but in the time-honoured fashion and taking

the easy option, the king came down in favour of the majority of monks and in turn he also decided that the defeated minority should be expelled from the city. As far as the king was concerned this was an admirable solution. If this happened there would certainly be no more disputes, no more rioting, and everything could return to normal. The only trouble was that the minority party would not budge – they would not leave the city as the king had ordered – and although he gave them several dire warnings if they continued to resist the royal decree, they still refused to leave. The king, in total exasperation, issued a further decree which said that any of the monks or their lay supporters who refused to comply with his order would be executed.

Of course, this ultimatum caused the utmost distress and consternation. It has to be understood that the monks of the minority party were well supported by a goodly number of lay followers who, whilst they could not follow the argument, at least were loyal to their chosen monks. So in the face of this dire threat the monks of the minority party, who had a good number of accepted arhats amongst their number, had a general meeting amongst themselves in order to decide what to do. After all, they were faced with only two choices: expulsion or death.

After some discussion they decided they would leave but leave in their own way and in their own time. They called in the representatives of their lay followers and asked them to assemble on the banks of the Ganges in the early morning of the date on which they were supposed to be executed. The time came and all the monks and their lay followers assembled on the banks of the Ganges and their arhat leaders gathered them all together and told them what they were going to do.

All the lay followers were rather surprised and not a little apprehensive at what they were told but the monks were recognised and acknowledged arhats and so they complied and closed their ranks into a tight circle. Whilst they were doing this they all heard the trumpets and drums of the military contingent which was approaching them to execute the king's orders. They had no time to lose!

When they were all gathered in a tight circle they were told to clasp each other around the waist. The arhats formed an outer circle around their lay followers and the arhats themselves joined hands. The whole gathering became a compact group. At the signal the arhats all together exercised their supernatural power and the entire body, monks and lay people, then rose into the air high above the capital and left the military with their mouths agape at the extraordinary spectacle. The arhats and their lay followers faced the North West and flew at high speed towards Kashmir, over a thousand miles away. All went well and they landed safely.

At this time Kashmir was a separate province from the rest of India and was outside that king's jurisdiction so the body of arhats and monks with their lay followers landed in Kashmir and over the next few years they gradually populated the area and finally they and their descendants completely converted Kashmir to Buddhism. It remained from then on a stronghold of the Sarvastivadin school of Indian Buddhism and was hugely influential in exporting the Dharma to all the countries around Kashmir, including central Asia and eventually to China.

This story is taken from *The Commentary on the Great Perfection of Wisdom.*

# THE APPEARANCE OF THE GREAT STUPA

then there
arose a stupa
consisting of
seven precious
substances
from the
place of
the earth

As the Buddha completed his great revelations on Vulture Peak an amazed hush fell over the huge assembly and then, in front of the place where the Buddha was seated, there arose out of the ground a great stupa. It emerged gradually, little by little: first of all the huge dome and then the enormous base with ascending levels. As the whole edifice emerged out of the ground and the massive dome and square base came fully into view, the whole structure rose high into the air and hovered there, seemingly completely unsupported.

The enormous stupa hovered high in the air well above the heads of all the assembly and when they had partly recovered from their astonishment, they saw that the stupa was covered with banners and flags and flower garlands of all colours and rows and rows of tinkling bells. From the stupa there issued a powerful voice saying, "Excellent, excellent, Lord Sakyamuni! Thou hast well expounded the Dharma, teaching of the Lotus of the True Dharma, indeed you have!"

On hearing these words everyone in the assembly rose up and extended their joined hands in front of them in salutation and then one of the great bodhisattvas present in the assembly, knowing the questions in the minds of all those present, asked the Buddha, "What is the cause of this and what produces these sounds emerging from the stupa?" The Buddha replied, "This stupa contains the remaining body of another buddha. This is his stupa and it is his voice that sounds from it". The Buddha continued, "This ancient buddha, called Prabhutaratna, at the end of his earthly life vowed that he would attend and appear and applaud any later buddha who expounded the Lotus Sutra." Having heard that answer, the same great bodhisattva asked again, "Using your great power, Lord, please show us the body of this ancient buddha." Sakyamuni Buddha replied, "Before doing that, it is proper that all the buddhas of the ten regions should gather here and witness this event," and so saying, he shone a bright ray of light from his forehead up into the sky and instantly all the buddha fields then appeared in plain view of everybody, each with its own buddha and his bodhisattvas and in all of them the Dharma was being preached. Sakyamuni Buddha employed his great powers again and created a host of jewelled trees around the stupa and the assembly and underneath each jewelled tree he placed a great throne. Then all those buddhas of the other worlds came down to this world and seated themselves on the great thrones under their appropriate trees. When all were seated, Sakyamuni Buddha rose up in the air and placed himself before the stupa. As he did this the whole assembly also rose, in great anticipation. Sakyamuni Buddha raised his right arm and, with his right forefinger, touched the latch. With a deep rumble the great double doors of the stupa opened and revealed the ancient buddha, Prabhutaratna, seated on a throne inside the stupa. His body was withered and emaciated but he repeated his approbation of the exposition of the Lotus Sutra and said he had come especially to hear it expounded.

When the ancient buddha had finished speaking he gestured to Sakyamuni Buddha, who was still standing in front of the Stupa, to join him and sit beside him on his throne. Sakyamuni Buddha accepted the invitation and moved into the stupa and sat next to the ancient buddha Prabhutaratna so both the present buddha and the ancient buddha sat side by side.

Everyone in the assembly then thought, "We cannot see the two buddhas inside the great stupa, they are too high up for us. If only we could rise to their level and see them both." Sakyamuni Buddha, knowing their wish, once more employed his supernatural powers and raised the entire assembly into the air, level with the great stupa, so that all could see the two buddhas seated there side by side. When all were raised up and could see properly, Sakyamuni Buddha said, "The end of my earthly appearance is approaching. I entrust this Lotus teaching to you all. Preserve it and pass it on to the rest of the world."

This story is taken from *The Lotus Sutra.*

# THE HIDDEN JEWEL

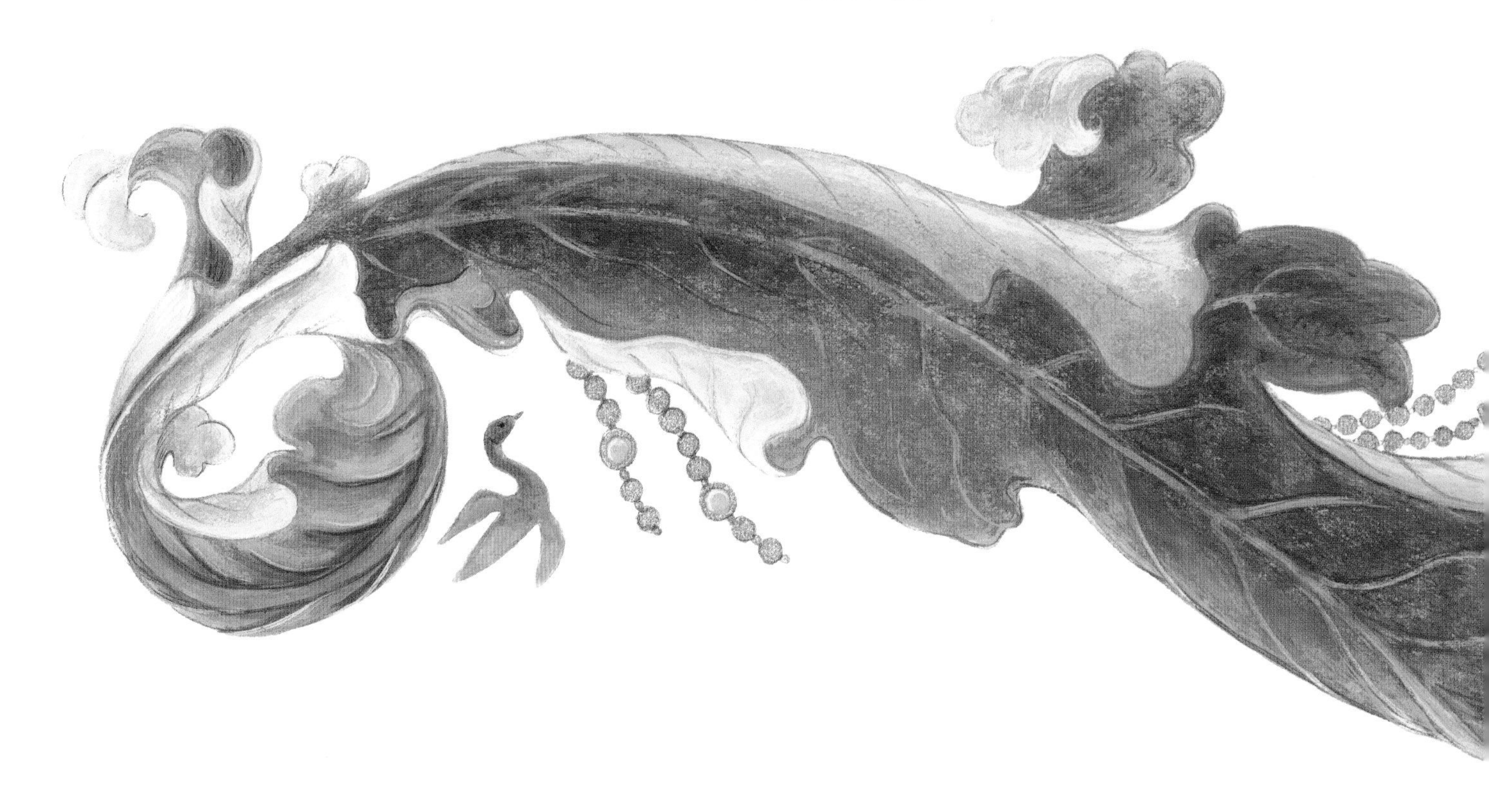

There was, in ancient India, a young man who was quite well off and who moved in a circle of equally well off friends and acquaintances. One day he went to visit one of them and a few others were there and the wine jar was passed around and they all had a very good time. In fact this young man had such a good time that he passed out, drunk.

His friends kindly laid him on a couch to recover but, being in very boisterous spirits, they began to conspire together. "He's out for the count! Well, now, what can we do? Can we play a trick on him?" Of course, the young man was lying absolutely drunk to the side and couldn't have cared less what they were doing to him so his friend said, "I know what we'll do. We'll take one of his jewels and we'll sew it into his clothes and then he'll miss it and hunt for it all over the place and he'll have it with him all the time. It'll be lovely. We'll watch him! Great stuff!" And they did this. They sewed a very valuable jewel into his garments.

When the young man awoke circumstances suddenly changed, as they often do, and he decided he was going to leave town to seek to better his 'fortune elsewhere (or was he was fed up with the partying?) Anyway, without even saying goodbye, he left. He went on long journeys, as merchants did in the course of business, but the farther he went, the worse things got for him. He couldn't do a thing right. He became poorer and poorer until, after some years of this wandering, he was utterly destitute. He'd lost all his business, everything. He had no friends and he was in a strange place. Nothing worked for him, all had failed and so he kept wandering.

His clothing was by now filthy and ragged and he was half-starved, stumbling and shambling. Eventually he came to a town and, in one of the streets of this town, he suddenly met his friend of the drunken party. How this friend could have recognised him is hard to know, but he did. The other one couldn't have recognised anybody, he was too far gone, but the friend, still very well-to-

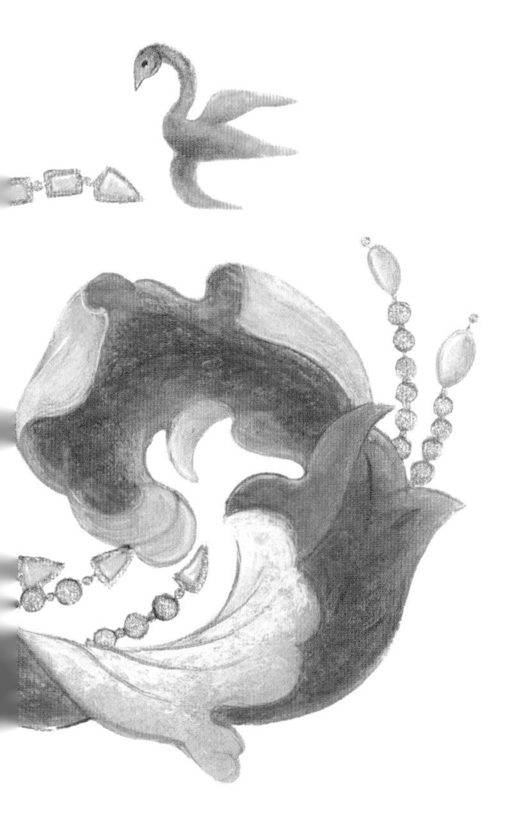

do and on a business trip, knew him, and stopped him in the street, and made himself known.

Of course, he was looked at with bleary, dull eyes, and he said, "What on earth has happened to you? Where have you been? What did you run off for? And what's been going on? How did you get into this state?" The man mumbled something about having bad luck, things just hadn't gone right, he'd felt too ashamed to come back again to his original home. The friend still couldn't understand. "But how did you get like this? I mean, look at you: you're filthy and you're smeared with dirt and grime and you look ill. Why haven't you taken better care of yourself?"

The man answered, "I've had nothing. I've been starving. I haven't eaten for days. I mean, what can I do?" The friend said, "Aren't you aware of what you're carrying around with you?" "What am I carrying around with me? All I've got is what I stand up in and that's not much: rags." "Don't you know you're carrying a priceless jewel in your undergarment?" "What? A priceless jewel? Where?"

And, of course, it had been sewn in his waistband and he found it and the first thing he did was to cry out, "Who played that trick on me? Where was that done? Why ever did you put it there? Why didn't you give it to me?" And the friend of the drunken party said, "Stop arguing about how you got it and when it got there. You've got it, it's there, go and spend it and get yourself better. Wash yourself, have a good meal and then come around and we'll have another party!"

This story is taken from *The Commentary on the Great Perfection of Wisdom.*

# BODHISATTVA EVER-WEEPING'S SEARCH FOR PERFECT WISDOM

*This tale was told by the Lord Buddha himself and it is truly a prince among stories.*

There was a disciple of the Lord Buddha called Sadaparudita, a high-sounding name but in fact all it means is Always-Weeping or Ever-Weeping or even Cry-Baby. He had been searching for years and years without cease for the Perfection of Wisdom. He went from place to place, teacher to teacher, always searching for it but never finding it.

One day, in his journeying, he was passing through a remote forest. As usual, he was commiserating with himself about how hard it was to find Perfect Wisdom. He slipped into a state of despondency, a common state for him, sat down and began to cry over his troubles. Suddenly there was a voice from the sky. This voice from the sky said to Ever-Weeping, "You should go east, young man. It is in the east that you shall find the Perfection of Wisdom. You might learn it from a book or you might learn it from a good friend but, whatever you do, shun all distractions and wrong paths. Be single-minded in your search in the east for Perfect Wisdom." The voice ceased.

Ever-Weeping was overjoyed. He had heard the Voice of Inspiration! He had actually been told where to go and what to do to find Perfect Wisdom! So off he went happily towards the east but gradually he started to wonder, "Where am I to go? How far east? Oh dear, I didn't ask a single question, oh dear." Immediately he plunged into great depths of despondency again and the tears came in floods. He had stopped dead in the middle of a desert and he was weeping and wailing and looking in all directions. "Who is going to help me? There's only me and I don't know where to go!"

This lamenting and crying and sobbing went on for seven days and for these seven days he ate no food and drank no water. He was utterly despondent and sat there, weeping and wailing. He must have been an expert weeper because the Buddha heard him and compassionately made a Buddha image to appear before him which said, "Your determination to seek Perfect Wisdom is very good, young man, but why are you crying? Why such a racket? Why are you all on your own in the middle of a desert crying your eyes out? Why don't you just get on with it?"

Ever-Weeping explained about the voice from the sky, and going east and all the rest of it and how he'd been too silly to even ask what place to head for. The Buddha image nodded and said, "Yes, I know how foolish you are but," he added, "this is a great thing you are undertaking. All the Buddhas of the past have searched for Perfect Wisdom with just the same zeal or more. This is the right thing to do. So, yes, you should go east. The voice was quite right. You should go five hundred leagues east to a city called Gandhavati."

In order to make quite sure that Ever-Weeping would recognise the place and not walk right through it and start crying again, he described the city in great detail. "Gandhavati is a prosperous and delightful town that is built of the seven precious things. It is enclosed by seven walls with seven moats and seven rows of trees. Between the trees there are strings of bells which give out a pretty tinkling sound all day long. It has an abundance of flowers, and pools of water, lakes and hundreds of shops full with a great variety of goods."

"In this city of Gandhavati is the mansion of the Bodhisattva Dharmodgata. It stands in the centre of the city at the crossing of four roads and the mansion is also enclosed by seven walls and seven rows of trees. The Bodhisattva Dharmodgata lives in this mansion with a great retinue of servants and ladies. The townsfolk enjoy and amuse themselves with all kinds of pleasures and the Bodhisattva Dharmodgata does likewise but regularly he demonstrates the Perfection of Wisdom. Now for this purpose," the Buddha image said to Ever-Weeping, "the townsfolk of Gandhavati have built

a splendid preaching platform for the Bodhisattva Dharmodgata. The platform has a solid gold base and it is piled with silks and cushions, sheltered by a high awning, with poles at each corner decorated all around the edges with pearls and from time to time the Bodhisattva Dharmodgata abandons his pleasures and his ladies and comes out to this platform and preaches the Perfection of Wisdom. At that time all the townsfolk also abandon their pleasures, whatever they are, and their occupations and they flock to the preaching platform and listen to Dharmodgata teaching. They listen with great respect, with trust in the Dharma and with hearts lifted up as a result of this bodhisattva's preaching and the townsfolk are joined in this by vast numbers of gods who also come to the city of Gandhavati and listen to the preaching of the Bodhisattva Dharmodgata. By doing this, all those beings of that city are blessed with great good fortune."

The Buddha image continued, "That is where you should go, Ever-Weeping. You should go to Gandhavati and you should seek out the Bodhisattva Dharmodgata. He has in fact been your good friend for a very long time. He has also searched for Perfect Wisdom as you now search for it. You should seek him out with all speed. Do not be diverted by anything else. Be assured that you will hear the Perfection of Wisdom from the great Bodhisattva Dharmodgata."

While the Buddha image was telling all this, Ever-Weeping was getting more and more enraptured. He was at last being given exact directions. He was being told that truly he would be able to find Perfect Wisdom, hearing all about it and understanding it, and as he listened he gradually acquired a state of total absorption, total concentration. Because of this concentration and the presence of the image of the Buddha he was able to see in the air all the buddhas of all the world systems. All of them were preaching Perfect Wisdom to countless numbers of bodhisattvas.

Ever-Weeping couldn't resist asking all these buddhas to confirm that his special good friend was the Bodhisattva Dharmodgata. "Is this really true?" All the buddhas noticed Ever-Weeping and they confirmed that Dharmodgata was his special friend, or, as he would be called in later times, his teacher, and they also told him that Dharmodgata had already taught and encouraged Ever-Weeping in the Path although Ever-Weeping had forgotten and that the Bodhisattva Dharmodgata was himself searching for Perfect Wisdom in his continuing path to full enlightenment and that Ever-Weeping's

search was of the same kind. Indeed, the very fact that Ever-Weeping was now searching for Perfect Wisdom at this moment was entirely due to the care and attention and teaching of the Bodhisattva Dharmodgata in previous existences, they told him, and that Bodhisattva Dharmodgata was well aware that Ever-Weeping was searching for him and was waiting to be found.

Ever-Weeping was utterly enraptured by all this but as soon as the buddhas had answered him they vanished and there was Ever-Weeping, alone again in the middle of this desert, surrounded by nothing but signs of his past tears. "Oh, oh, where have they all gone? Why am I left alone here? What do I do now? I'm alone in the desert again. They told me where to go but how do I start? Which way?" The tears started again. He wailed, "I have to find the Bodhisattva Dharmodgata and since I am his predestined pupil I have to take him a present but I have nothing! How can I manage to get my teacher a present? What am I to do?" The weeping increased. "How terrible, I don't know where to go nor what to do. How will I cope, all alone like this! It's too much!"

After some more sobbing and wailing, it occurred to him that if he didn't get out of this desert quickly and find some food, water and shelter he wouldn't be searching for anything much longer. So he set off, due east.

After travelling about halfway along the route to Gandhavati, Ever-Weeping entered a small market town, something like a caravan town on the old Silk Road. There he thought, "I must find a gift for Bodhisattva Dharmodgata. I can't go empty-handed. This is probably my last chance to find something because there may be no more towns on the way." Then he had what he considered a really bright idea. "There is only one thing I possess and that is myself so I will offer myself for sale."

He went into the centre of the market square and started to call out, over and over, "Who wants to buy a man? Man for sale!" He was sure that he wouldn't have to shout this for very long, he was bound to find a taker in this town. However, his cry was heard by the god Mara the Malign, who didn't like the sound of it at all. He exercised a power that prevented everyone from hearing anything Ever-Weeping was saying. Ever-Weeping was of course unaware of this and kept on calling out and he got more and more frustrated and more and more worried until he burst into tears again. "Here I'm fit and capable of doing anything and with the money I'd get I could buy something for Dharmodgata but I'm getting nowhere!" Floods of tears streamed down again.

This time the tears woke up Sakra, King of Gods. So first, all the Buddhas, then Mara, now Sakra. What a nuisance! Sakra, hearing all this weeping and wailing, took on the form of a young merchant. "This racket is driving me daft. I must find out what this bloke's on about."

Down he went to the market square and confronted Ever-Weeping. "Are you really offering yourself for sale?" "Of course I am," replied Ever-Weeping between sobs, "because I want to buy a present for my teacher, the Bodhisattva Dharmodgata."

"We must test this fellow," thought Sakra. "After all Bodhisattva Dharmodgata doesn't want to be bothered with just anybody, particularly with anybody who keeps bursting into tears. We'll just see if this chap is serious." So Sakra said to Ever-Weeping, "Well now, young man, your proposition is of interest to me. It so happens that my family is about to set up a special sacrifice, one of profound import, from which we will derive great benefit but for that sacrifice I shall need a man's heart, blood and marrow. You are, after all, offering yourself for sale. Are you prepared to sell your heart, blood and marrow?"

Ever-Weeping said, "Of course, but first, what will you give for it?" He may have been weepy but he wasn't stupid. So they had a little haggle there in the marketplace over the price until Ever-Weeping accepted an offer and then Sakra stood back and said, "Right. Let's have it." Ever-Weeping looked about and finally asked, "Have you got a knife or something?" Sakra said, "Here, have my sword." So Ever-Weeping began slicing flesh off his arm and then off his thigh and, of course, instead of tears flowing all over the place, it was blood.

"Stop, stop," cried a horrified voice and there rushing into the square was a young lady. "Don't do that terrible thing," she cried. "Look what you are doing to yourself. Whatever are you up to? And see the mess!" She was in quite a passion over the mess. Ever-Weeping stopped immediately and even Sakra lost no time in vanishing.

The young lady, the daughter of a merchant whose mansion bordered the square, had been sitting in her window like all highbred ladies, observing the passing scene and looking nice. And as she watched, she saw Ever-Weeping start to slice his flesh. Without thinking a moment, she ran downstairs and into the square to put a stop to this. Now she demanded to know what he was doing and why he was doing it. Ever-Weeping explained about needing a gift for the great teacher in Gandhavati who was going to instruct him in the Perfection of Wisdom. "I had just arranged to sell my heart, blood and bones to that fellow and was starting to slice off a bit of flesh and now he's gone!"

The merchant's daughter said to him, "Well, if that's all you're worried about, just having the means to buy a gift, I'll see that you get it! Just stop making a mess of our beautiful square. And, what's more, I know the way to Gandhavati. It's the next city on this road and I will be glad to go with you. I am most interested in what you've told me about the Bodhisattva Dharmodgata. I'll provide everything."

At this, Sakra reappeared in his true form. Praising Ever-Weeping's determination to carry out the bargain, he healed the wounds Ever-Weeping had made slicing off his flesh and then offered, "Choose whatever you want and I will give it to you." "There is only one thing I want, Sakra, and that is the Buddha faculties." "Oh no, that is quite beyond me. I can give you anything else but not those. No, son, you are on your own." And with that he vanished again.

After his disappearance, Ever-Weeping and the merchant's daughter discussed how to make the next stage of the journey to Gandhavati. She, as a dutiful daughter, said, "Look, I must first ask my parents if I can go." "Well, yes, that is quite right," agreed Ever-Weeping. They crossed the square to

her house and the girl said to him, "I think you had better stay outside, for if my parents see you in that state they might get a terrible shock. So I shall go in and explain all to them in a way they can accept. I'll try to persuade them but you stay there and wait until I come and tell you all's well or not."

The merchant's daughter went inside, found her parents and, coming to the point straight away, asked them for her portion of the family's wealth. She needed it, she said, so that she could go off with Ever-Weeping to Gandhavati to meet the Bodhisattva Dharmodgata. Of course, Father and Mother said, "Wait a minute, who is this Ever-Weeping? Who is this Bodhisattva Dharmodgata? Why on earth do you want to do this?" They were very upset.

Their daughter told them the story from start to finish: that Ever-Weeping was searching for Perfect Wisdom and was so determined that he had been in the process of self-mutilation and he had been told that Bodhisattva Dharmodgata was in the city of Gandhavati teaching Perfect Wisdom and that Perfect Wisdom leads to the full enlightenment of a Buddha. "And besides," she added, "Ever-Weeping, obviously, is also a great bodhisattva, worthy of honour, and so is the Bodhisattva Dharmodgata worthy of honour. I would much like to pay my respects to the Bodhisattva Dharmodgata in the company of Ever-Weeping. After all, we don't often meet bodhisattvas in this little market town, do we, Mum?"

Mum and Dad were very impressed that a great bodhisattva, worthy of honour, was actually standing on their doorstep waiting for them and thought, "What a very good opportunity." And Mother said, "Your father and I aren't doing anything just now as it happens. We'll also come along with you." Daughter was delighted. "Wonderful! Let's go right away!" She ran outside to the waiting Ever-Weeping and told him the good news.

The entire household was mobilised for the journey. They were a very rich family: the daughter alone had five hundred handmaidens! The whole household was packed up with their goods and chattels on five hundred horse-drawn carts. All the pots and pans and tables and chairs and beds were piled up in a long row of these carts, each with its retinue of servants. In front was a carriage in which sat the merchant's daughter and Ever-Weeping, behind them the parents' carriage and then the long row of wagons with the servants. Off they went to see the bodhisattva. The happy caravan travelled east: Ever-Weeping and the merchant's daughter, her parents, their servants and all their possessions in the carts behind them along the desert road. In time they reached Gandhavati. There the party passed through the gates of all the seven walls and entered the city. They approached the centre, the main square, and found assembled there the population of the whole town, massed around the preaching platform. On it was the Bodhisattva Dharmodgata, preaching to them.

Ever-Weeping and the merchant's daughter alighted from their carriage and, accompanied by the lady's five hundred handmaidens, approached the platform. There they saw, at the back of the platform, created especially by the Bodhisattva Dharmodgata for this Dharma teaching, a great pointed tower made of the seven precious materials, lots of red sandalwood and pearls. Ever-Weeping and the young lady could see that the tower was attended all around by countless gods scattering heavenly flowers over it. Other gods were playing music, all honouring the bodhisattva and the great tower.

Ever-Weeping noticed that Sakra was there. He went up to the god and asked him why the tower was so specially honoured. Sakra explained that inside the tower in the middle of the ground floor was an empty couch and, on this couch, a jewelled box. Inside the jewelled box was the text of the Perfection of Wisdom Sutra, written upon golden tablets. This was a cause for great honour, he said, and the reason for the gods' attendance and their special flowers and music. On hearing this and seeing the gods, the tower and the bodhisattva, Ever-Weeping, the merchant's daughter, her parents, and all the servants offered flowers and garlands and jewels and incense from the goods they had brought with them and scattered flowers over Dharmodgata. As they scattered these flowers over his head, the blossoms formed up into the exact shape of the tower that stood behind. And all the jewels and garlands that they also offered rose high in the air to form a pavilion in the sky.

Now all this happened even before Ever-Weeping and the merchant's daughter had heard a word of the preaching. They were still intent on paying honour and respect. They and their servants were struck with wonder at the power of the great bodhisattva, even before he attained enlightenment. The merchant's daughter and her handmaidens were particularly moved by awe and wonder and longing: so moved that they felt that they wanted to be like the Bodhisattva Dharmodgata and, like him, embark on the path to full enlightenment. This is

raising the aspiration towards enlightenment. Ever-Weeping approached the bodhisattva with profound salutations, introduced himself and recounted his story, starting with the voice in the sky in the middle of the desert. The bodhisattva, although of course knowing all about it, listened with the greatest patience to the whole tale. Then Ever-Weeping came to the point. The Buddha image in the desert, he said, had assured him that Bodhisattva Dharmodgata was his special good friend and that through his care and attention Ever- Weeping would learn and acquire Perfect Wisdom. "But before that," Ever-Weeping said, "I want to know, please, where did all those buddhas in the sky come from and where did they all go to?"

"Buddhas do not come or go anywhere," Dharmodgata replied. "Just as dreams are illusory and can't be said to arrive or depart, so a mirage can't be said to have arisen or departed because it is never there anyway. That is the illusory part of it," and he continued a preaching which, although Ever-Weeping didn't yet realise it, was exactly what he'd come all this way for. He asked something else, "Where do buddhas come from?" but in fact the answer he got was Perfect Wisdom. In response to this preaching, the whole earth shook. The earth always shakes when certain events of huge moment take place. When the Buddha was about to be enlightened the earth shook. And here also the earth shook.

Dharmodgata then said to Ever-Weeping that thousands of beings had gained insight from Ever-Weeping's question and its answer. These thousands were now inspired to long for full enlightenment and to embark on the path towards it. This was another reason why the earth shook, he said. Ever-Weeping was overjoyed to hear that such a wonderful thing had come about as a result of their exchange and then he began to realise the full scope of what had taken place. He became aware of what was going on at that moment over, above, underneath and around their meeting and he was enraptured, so much so that he rose to the height of seven palm trees and sat there, looking down.

Dharmodgata wasn't the least bit surprised by this: he often sat up at the height of seven palm trees himself. He knew there was nothing unusual about this but the merchant's daughter didn't. She was in utter bewilderment. Seven palm trees! Sitting up there and obviously liking it!

While Ever-Weeping sat there, Sakra, King of the Gods, approached him and offered him heavenly flowers so that he could scatter them on Dharmodgata. Ever-Weeping did so until his shadow fell across Dharmodgata. At that moment Ever- Weeping came down from the height of seven palm trees and, standing in front of the bodhisattva, offered himself. This was his gift. Although he had gone to great lengths to acquire a gift to give Dharmodgata, when the time came, the gift he gave was himself. All other gifts were forgotten. He offered himself to Dharmodgata as his servant and slave and then stood to one side. The merchant's daughter and her servants, seeing this, also came forward and they too gave themselves, not to Dharmodgata, but to Ever- Weeping. They offered themselves as a gift and promised to honour all the buddhas with him throughout the whole length of his path. Ever- Weeping accepted this gift of themselves to him as an earnest reflection of his own offering himself to Bodhisattva Dharmodgata. Sakra, in the wings all the time, applauded and stated that all bodhisattvas must renounce all their possessions. Dharmodgata accepted the gift of Ever- Weeping and by so doing accepted Ever-Weeping and all those that belonged to him, the merchant's daughter and her servants, so as to fulfil the good intention with which the gift was made. A gift has to be completed, offered, given and accepted, if the intention is to be carried out. Dharmodgata accepted all the gifts and immediately returned them to Ever-Weeping and withdrew into his house. At that instant the sun set. Darkness descended.

Ever-Weeping resolved to remain standing or walking until the bodhisattva should come out again. There are four kinds of posture: standing, walking, lying and sitting. Ever-Weeping resolved to keep only two of those postures, standing and walking, the most exhausting. He would not sit or lie down until Dharmodgata reappeared. The merchant's daughter and her handmaidens made exactly the same resolution. They would follow him. They would do exactly as he did.

Ever-Weeping remained in a state of absorption, a state of Dhyana, for seven years. Throughout that time he experienced only the continuous desire for Dharmodgata to return and preach. After seven years the voice from the sky again spoke to Ever-Weeping. It announced that Dharmodgata was about to return, about to emerge again from his house, in seven days' time. All the proper preparations must be made. Ever-Weeping and the merchant's daughter and the five hundred maids were overjoyed. They immediately began to clean up. Out came the brooms. They swept the square clean and laid everything in its proper place. They prepared the platform on which the bodhisattva would appear, spreading on it their own upper garments.

Ever-Weeping realised that, having swept everywhere, the dust had to be laid with a sprinkling of water. He searched around for water and this process once again awakened Mara. "It's Ever-Weeping again," he thought. "Doesn't he ever learn?" He removed all the water. There was none to be found!

Ever-Weeping, determined that everything should be right for the reappearance of the Bodhisattva took a sharp sword and wounded himself so that his blood could be spread on the square to settle the dust. The merchant's daughter and her servants did the same, so there were lashings of blood everywhere. Sakra appeared again and applauded their resolve. "How marvellous," he said, "to see you so intent on your preparations!" and he changed the blood to sandalwood powder, which spread a wonderful aroma all over the square and for miles around. He also provided Ever-Weeping with heavenly flowers again for spreading on the ground and for sprinkling over the bodhisattva when the time came.

After seven days the square was prepared and the platform was ready. Out came Dharmodgata. He emerged from his own meditations, mounted the platform and took his seat. He then preached at length on the special qualities of the Perfection of Wisdom for which Ever-Weeping had searched for so long. Ever-Weeping was filled with rapture to see him and hear him speak. After all he had waited for seven years.

This time there was no delivery of Perfect Wisdom by analogy. Now he actually preached directions on the subject of Perfect Wisdom, for which Ever-Weeping had been searching over many lives. As a result of hearing it, Ever-Weeping acquired the most exalted states of purified wisdom. With each word that he heard, his intense, concentrated

and purified state increased and heightened. There came to him such great wisdom and sublime concentration that, although in entirely different circumstances, he once again was able to see all the Buddhas of the ten directions, each surrounded by an entire retinue of bodhisattvas and those Buddhas were preaching to their bodhisattvas in the same words as Dharmodgata was preaching to Ever-Weeping. The whole universe was full of Buddhas preaching the same words.

Ever-Weeping never again suffered rebirth into the lower realms. Having found and gained the Perfection of Wisdom, he could never lose it. In all his later existences, he was always face to face with the Buddhas, even in his dreams. He eventually became a great bodhisattva who serves all beings and leads them to Perfect Wisdom just as he himself was led and just as the Bodhisattva Dharmodgata had led him. He now had no further cause to weep and cry his eyes out but he retained the name, Ever-Weeping, to remind everyone of how his search had started.

This story is taken from *The Perfection of Wisdom in 8000 Lines.*

# THE ARHAT AND THE NUN'S JAR

Somewhere in India, not long after the death of the Lord Buddha, probably somewhere north of the Ganges Basin where he would have made his visits, there was a monk called Upagupta. Upagupta was in fact an arhat, which is to say that he had travelled the path to its end, laid down the burden and attained Nirvana, as the Buddha instructed.

Now this monk Upagupta was very interested – no, fervently, devotionally interested – in the Buddha himself. He was avid to know exactly what the Buddha did, how he did it, how he looked, what sort of things he said, how he impressed people, so he sought out anyone who might have heard stories about him from the Buddha's own lifetime. Finally, he learned of a nun who was one hundred and five years old and had been ordained during the life of the Lord Buddha. This person would be able to tell him all he needed to know since she had attended him personally!

The zealous monk discovered that the nun now lived alone in a little hut outside a nearby town so he immediately sent an emissary, another monk, to tell her that the great arhat Upagupta was about to come to find out all she knew about the activities and general disposition of the Lord Buddha. When the nun heard this, she replied only, "Yes, that's fine. He can come if he wants. I shall be here."

On the day appointed, the nun made her preparations. The doorway to her hut was covered by a hanging screen made of reeds which allowed air to enter, of course, but prevented anyone outside from seeing in. Just inside the entrance, just a little bit to one side of the screen, she placed a bowl full of oil. Then she composed herself and waited for the arrival of the great arhat Upagupta.

He came as expected and strode through the doorway, as arhats do. The bowl of oil went flying. "Oh, yes. Oh, yes," said the nun.

She paid him the respect due one of his station, providing a seat, and water to wash his feet. Then they sat for a while and Upagupta asked her question after question about the Lord Buddha: how he looked and how he had acted. She answered fully but when he had finished she said, "Now I will tell you something from the time of the Lord Buddha that you probably don't know about. When I was there with him, there were six monks who were most unruly and always had to be disciplined. They couldn't be trusted for five minutes! If they were out of sight, they were in trouble all the time but," she continued, "those six monks came to visit me and not one of them knocked over my bowl of oil."

"So that's the first thing. Next," she went on, "I will tell you something else you probably don't know about, and which I treasure from that day to this.

When I was a young woman, not yet ordained, not yet a nun, still in my teens, I went to hear the Lord Buddha preach. I was dressed in all my finery with my hair piled high and held by jewelled hairpins. There were lots of people there, of course, and when I came to where the Lord Buddha was, I bowed to him and as I did that, one of my beautiful hairpins fell out of my hair and into the undergrowth at my feet. I couldn't find it, I thought I'd lost it and I started to scrabble about. This is the kind of thing the Lord Buddha does: he saw me scrabbling for my hairpin and he directed the glorious rays from his halo onto the ground in front of me so that the hairpin sparkled. I could see it sparkle so I was able to find it and put it back into my hair. That was enough for me. I took refuge in the Lord Buddha."

And then she said again, "The unruly monks weren't even arhats and yet they did not overturn my bowl of oil. An arhat should know better. You should be more careful. You should know there's a bowl of oil behind the screen. The Lord Buddha was always careful. Whatever he did, he exercised the utmost care while you, as an arhat, you just barge in through my door and upset my oil! Go!"

The arhat went, covered in shame, but he went with the utmost care.

This story is taken from *The Commentary on the Great Perfection of Wisdom.*

# THE OLD WOMAN WHO COULDN'T SEE THE BUDDHA

The Lord Buddha and Ananda were walking through a small town one day, begging for food most probably, when in the distance they saw an elderly woman standing at the door of her house. "Look," said Ananda, "such a worthy person! What a good opportunity to spread the Dharma! Will you give her some teaching?" "No," the Buddha replied. "There is no way at all that I can have a meeting with that person. Not in this life, nor in her previous existences has she planted sufficient roots of right conduct."

Ananda, a soft-hearted person, pressed the Buddha to show compassion for her. "Ananda," said the Buddha, "you don't seem to understand the situation. Anything I might try to do for that woman would be useless because she wouldn't even be able to see me near her. How can I teach the Dharma to someone incapable of seeing that I am here?"

They continued walking but Ananda was dumbstruck by this remark. Finally, he said, "How can she not see that you're here? I don't understand that." The Buddha answered, "It is a very rare thing for human beings to be able to see the Buddha. I shall show you how rare it is. You stay put."

The Buddha approached the woman. As he walked toward her and came very close, she turned her back on him. It wasn't that she saw him and didn't want to meet him, it was just that she was sweeping and had to turn around to do her work. That was the reason.

The Buddha then called out to Ananda to watch carefully. He walked right in front of her and again her sweeping required her to turn away. She continued doing what she was doing regardless of the Buddha's presence. Obviously, she didn't see him. He then levitated over her head and looked down on her. Sweeping away, she was concentrating on her feet. So the Buddha sank to the ground and came up between her feet. But just then, unaware of him, she happened to be staring at the sky and failed to notice.

He performed more feats like these, approaching her from all directions. He even multiplied himself until she was encircled by a dozen Buddhas all around her. She carried on as before, not seeing any of them.

Finally the Buddha withdrew. "There are some people," he said, "who, even in the lifetime of the Buddha, even face to face with the Buddha, even surrounded by the Buddha, cannot see him. Do you understand now, Ananda?"

This story is taken from *The Commentary on the Great Perfection of Wisdom*.

THE MAGIC CITY

Long ago in ancient India, travel of any kind to any place was a matter of extreme danger and discomfort, at the very least. There was no such thing as a pleasant journey, not even for the most august and powerful. A journey was, for anyone, a matter of apprehension and fear and, "Let's hope the gods smile on our enterprise!" Astrologers were called in to make sure the trip started on the right day, otherwise disaster. And, of course, the most dangerous journeys were those that didn't follow the established routes, the highways with staging posts and rest houses.

So the usual practice was to hire a reliable guide. And a story is told about a party of merchants and pilgrims and sons returning home, most of them carrying precious jewels and other valuable goods and all in great fear of bandits and robbers. The guide they hired was not only experienced and reliable, he also was known as a wizard, a magician. He had travelled that route many times and knew every inch of the way. He also knew that at the end of their journey they hoped to reach the City of Pearls.

The way to this city led them through the most atrocious terrain, so thick and black that sunlight could not penetrate. It was infested with all kinds of wild animals, there was no drinkable water, it was hot and steamy and the path had to be hacked out. The magician knew that this stretch was the hardest but possible, although he had his doubts about this group. They pushed on during the day but at night they had to light fires to keep the roaring animals at bay and they were terrified of the snakes and the other wild beasts. They weren't getting any sleep at all and this went on for several days and nights.

So there came a time when they were completely exhausted. Their guide realised that they wouldn't finish their journey unless they stopped but he also realised that to stop in this place was to stop for good. The only way out was to press on. His problem was that his party were too weak to travel but sure to die if they stopped. Fortunately, he was a magician of extraordinary powers. He said to them that although they had not yet reached the City of Pearls, they had done very,very well so far. And, he added, luckily there was a town nearby, not on the map but just a slight diversion, where they could rest awhile and prepare for the final leg of the journey. The travellers were delighted.

He led them down a by-path ... and there was this gorgeous little town! Clear water, open houses, pools, lakes, parks, friendly villagers coming to welcome them. "How great," everyone thought, "our struggles are over!" They stretched out by the bathing pool, sipping long cool drinks, everything at hand. The strains and rigours of the journey faded, they forgot the jungle and there was no thought at all of the City of Pearls.

The magician, however, knew that every member of the party had a reason for getting there. Important documents had to be delivered, money handed over, families rejoined after years of absence. But the travellers, having had such a hard time and enjoying themselves so much now, were too worn out. They had forgotten the reasons for going on the journey.

The magician decided there was only one thing to do. Without warning, he made the whole town vanish, in an instant. It was only a conjured, magical city anyway, that he'd created. The travellers were shocked! No pool, no drinks, just themselves lying on the ground in an open plain without houses or parks or trees. No anything. It had all been a mirage. The magician explained that it had been his creation, he'd made it for them, but because it was time to travel on again, he'd destroyed it. They were furious!

He silenced the anger by asking them how they felt after stopping in the beautiful town for a while. "Three days ago you were exhausted and unable to walk another step. Now you're rested, restored. Now we can actually reach the City of Pearls. Now, it's not too far away. Before it was completely out of your reach."

They knew he was right. They knew they could get there. Then they remembered their reasons for going and set off happily.

They made it.

This story is taken from *The Lotus Sutra*.

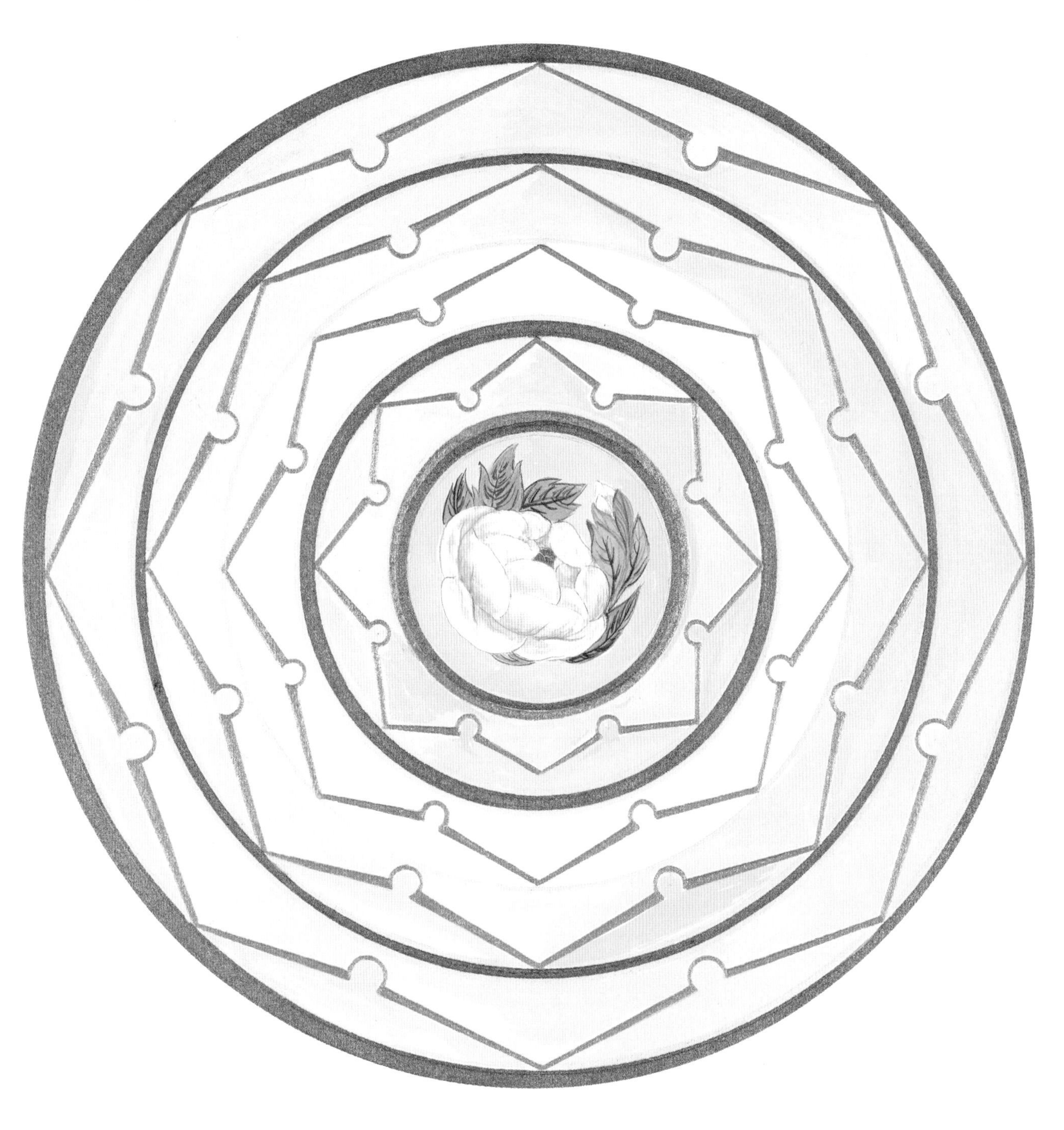

# THE LOST SON

There was, long ago, an Indian merchant of princely wealth and power. He had but one child, a son, and this boy was so precious to his parents that they quite naturally reared him in cushioned comfort, with servants waiting to meet his every need. It was also quite natural that as he grew, his self-confidence grew too until it was boundless, until he was sure that he knew all there was to know about everything. Indeed, he became sure that he knew much more than his father, whom he privately regarded as something of a bully, and certainly more than his mother, who seemed to him to be a weakling. So the day came when he decided to leave home and show them that without any help he could become just as rich as his father. He defiantly set out on his own and disappeared from their lives.

Years passed and the grieving parents heard nothing of him. The father, like many another merchant of the time, travelled widely in the course of his trade but, unlike the other merchants, he was also constantly searching for his lost son. Because of their great wealth, the family had many vast estates around the country, each with fine palaces and parks and gardens. The father moved from one to the next in great state, in a caravan of carriages drawn by plumed horses, with servants and guards and all the household necessities and with elephants bearing trunks of jewels, silks and other precious things. It was an imposing, even intimidating procession.

One day, his carriage paused at the gates of one of these opulent palaces to let the servants sweep the entrance. The father stepped down from his carriage and, as he did, his eyes fell on a filthy beggar who was gazing with awe at the glittering caravan. The father instantly recognised in the ruined face his own son, his lost son.

At that moment, the beggar's expression changed to fear and he turned and fled. The excited, joyful father immediately ordered his guards to go after him and bring him back but the fleeing beggar, in a passion of fear, believed himself to have angered a king. After years of failure, then poverty and finally beggary, he no longer remembered his father's face. He had forgotten his own high origins, he had forgotten his beautiful home. His only thought now was that the king's men, these terrifying fighters hard on his heels with their jewelled swords and daggers at their gleaming belts, were about to kill him. So he ran for his life.

He was caught and dragged, crying and screaming, back to the palace gates. "Let me go," he begged, "I'm innocent! I've done nothing!" His terror was palpable. The father saw all this and saw the profound fear gripping him. He knew it could kill him. He ordered his guards to let him go. The beggar fled into the village alleyways. The father realised that although he had found his beloved son, his lost child, there could be no reunion, no homecoming in the presence of this fear. So he ordered his guards to change their uniforms for filthy, tattered work clothes and find the beggar. They were then to befriend him and offer him work, any work that he was willing to do. Above all, they were to stay with him.

The guards did as they were bid. In the guise of lowly workers they found the frightened man in the next village and fell to chatting with him. He was recovering from his terror, feeling lucky to be alive, and agreed readily when his new friends suggested he come along to a place where all of them could find work. They took him to the outhouses of his father's estate, avoiding the main gates so that he wouldn't recognise where he was. Then he was told that the work would be easy and regular, the pay good, and the master fair and generous.

He was set to sweeping the yards, to cleaning up all the muck and dirt and dung. The man was delighted: this kind of work he'd been doing for years wherever he could find it but here he could do it over and over again in the same place and,

# the parable of the lost son

when night fell, a corner of a pigsty for his own! He swept faithfully and diligently, quite content. He didn't care for whom he swept all this muck, so long as each night he was safe and unafraid.

After many months of patient observation, the merchant decided on a move. He, too, took off his silken robes and jewelled headdress and put on the tattered rags of a workman. Smearing his face with grime, he went down into the yard and swept muck beside his son. In time, they began to talk. The disguised father said he was the head sweeper, in charge of all sweepers. "Have no fear," he said. "I've watched you for some time and I know that you're a good worker. I just wanted to make myself known to you. I will continue to watch you and occasionally lend a hand, so don't try to play any tricks." The son accepted this news quite calmly and the two settled into a peaceful relationship, the father coming often in his work clothes to sweep beside his son, chatting amiably.

Years went by like this. The father persisted with great patience in his role as comradely supervisor. He saw that at first the younger man was unafraid only when sweeping busily in his familiar yard, alone. If a guard, or a stranger, or anyone from the estate approached, he would flee in fear into the pigsty. As time passed, he became gradually, slowly, less fearful, until he could talk to fellow workers without signs of panic.

One day the father decided that the moment for another move had come. He now changed his disguise to that of the master, not sumptuously rich as he truly was, but moderately wealthy. He dispatched an aide to the yard to bring the grimy sweeper before him. At this novel summons, the son was flooded with anxiety. "Have I done wrong?" he wondered. "I must have done something terribly wrong for the master to want to see me!" Even though he knew his master to have been fair with him throughout all these years, and, according to the friendly supervisor, very satisfied with his work, he was still terrified of anything unknown, but of course he went with the aide, suffering torments of fear and anxiety.

However, this is what his master said, "I've been watching your work, my man, and I can see that you're honest and diligent. You can be trusted. I value such servants. Now I want you to do something different. I am growing old and I have no son to carry on my affairs so I am going to show you how to look after my counting house, my ingoings and outgoings. We'll see how you get on with it and we'll give you

very good training. When I see that you're fully competent and well able for it, not before, I will want you to take on full responsibility."

The son was overjoyed that he wasn't to be punished for some unknown crime. So he entered training as a steward. For this he cleaned himself up but each night he returned to his pigsty. In time, he became adept at the work and earned his master's confidence. He was consulted more and more on financial questions. After years of steady growth, he became chief steward, in charge of all the estate. His master was full of praise for his soundness and reliability but even so, the son suffered keen anxiety before every encounter with him, still frightened. He felt always on trial, unsure of who he was. And still, every night, and even though now the chief steward, he crept into his sty to sleep.

By now, his father felt himself growing old. It saddened him to see his son, so successful at his work, still separated from his rightful place, living in the pigsty. He called the younger man to him, therefore, and instructed him to organise a public gathering in the main courtyard. He must invite all the people of the estates, all of the townspeople and anyone else having business with the family. There was to be a most important announcement.

The day came and the father put off the mundane clothing, suited to the master of an ordinary estate, and dressed again in sumptuous silks and jewelled headdress. When all were gathered in the courtyard, he entered in majestic procession and took his place on a throne upon a dais. His chief steward, recognising him, fell upon his knees. He listened without fear to his father's words.

"The time has come to appoint a successor to my fortunes. Every man would hope to pass his estates to his son. For a long time it has been thought that there is no son in this family, but in fact this is not true. Many years ago I had a son. This son left his home and became lost to me. After long searching, however, he was found and although he did not know me then, he will know me now. We have worked side by side on these estates for decades. He has learned to trust me and so when I now tell him, my chief steward, who he really is, he will believe me. He is my lost son and he must now rise up and take his place beside me on this dais."

No longer afraid, the son arose and joined his father. He knew where he belonged. When night fell, he slept at home.

This story is taken from *The Lotus Sutra.*

# THE RAIN CLOUD

"That was an excellent story but it only illustrates a part of what I was saying", the Lord Buddha said to the arhat who had just finished relating the story of the lost son. "What I had in mind was rather different. All the Buddhas and the Dharma teaching they expound all their lives are like a great rain cloud."

He was talking about India and the Monsoon. It is not an occasional shower but a great black cloud that covers entire areas and the rain pours down in floods, not just briefly but lasting for days.

The Buddha continued, "All the Buddhas and the Dharma teaching are like a great rain cloud. It gathers itself together and it pours down life-giving rain onto the land, which has been parched for the whole season, and the rain falls everywhere indiscriminately. It doesn't care whether it is on a house, or a town, or a river, on a field, on a mountain, on the sea. It doesn't care. It all falls equally, everywhere and the plants absorb it, it is their life-blood, and the animals drink but the rocks can do nothing, it just runs off their backs. But the rain still pours down. That is what I mean."

This story is taken from *The Lotus Sutra*.

# A SIMPLIFIED GLOSSARY

*Abhidharma* Higher knowledge
*Ananda* The Buddha's attendant and one of his chief disciples
*Arhat* A Buddhist saint who has completed the Path
*Asoka* Buddhist emperor who reigned in India two hundred years after the death of the Buddha
*Bactria* A region of Central Asia now lying in Afghanistan, Uzbekistan and Tajikistan
*Bharadvaja Pindola* A prominent monk-disciple of the Buddha who displayed super-normal powers
*Bodhisattva* A being who is oriented towards full enlightenment
*Brahma* A great god
*Buddha Faculties* The special faculties of a buddha, of which there are eighteen
*Buddha-field* The sphere of influence of a given bodhisattva or buddha
*Buddhist Order* Ordained monks and nuns
*Caravanserai* A desert staging post for caravans
*Central Asia* The core region of the Asian continent, stretching from the Caspian Sea in the west to China in the east and from Afghanistan in the south to Russia in the north
*Cintamani* The wish-fulfilling gem
*City of Pearls* Enlightenment
*Concentration on Goodwill* A meditation practice to develop compassion
*Concentration on Space* A deep meditation on Sunyata
*Crest Jewel* See Cintamani
*Dais* A raised platform
*Devi* A goddess
*Dharma*
  *The Dharma* The Buddha's teaching
  *A dharma* One of the ultimate elements of existence
*Dharmakaya* The corpus of the whole teaching
*Dhyana* Ordinary meditation
*Ganges* A great river flowing through northern India and Bangladesh
*Great Way* The Way to full enlightenment
*Heaven of the Thirty Three* The home of Sakra
*Himalayas* A mountain range which separates the Indian Subcontinent from Tibet
*Homily* A story with a purpose
*Kalpa* A long period of time
*Kashmir* An area spanning the border of India and Pakistan
*Kathina* A Buddhist festival day when lay people present the monks with their new bowls, clothing and bedding
*Laity* Householders
*Lotus Blossom* A flower that is a symbol of purity as it is rooted in mud but flowers above the water
*Lotus Sutra* One of the first scriptures of the Mahayana, the 'further teaching'
*Mahasattva* A great being who is a high-ranking bodhisattva
*Mahayana* A more advanced teaching of Buddhism contained in the first written sutras
*Manjusri* The great bodhisattva of wisdom
*Mara* A divinity of the sensuous realm
*Maudgalyayana* An eminent arhat and one of the two chief disciples of the Buddha
*Mind-Made* Subjective
*Miracle of the Fire and Water* The 'twin miracle' in which the Buddha rose into the air and simultaneously emitted fire and water from his body
*Mount Meru* The pivot or axis of the world and abode of the gods
*Naga Kingdom* The underwater realm of water serpents or dragons which is filled with magnificent palaces

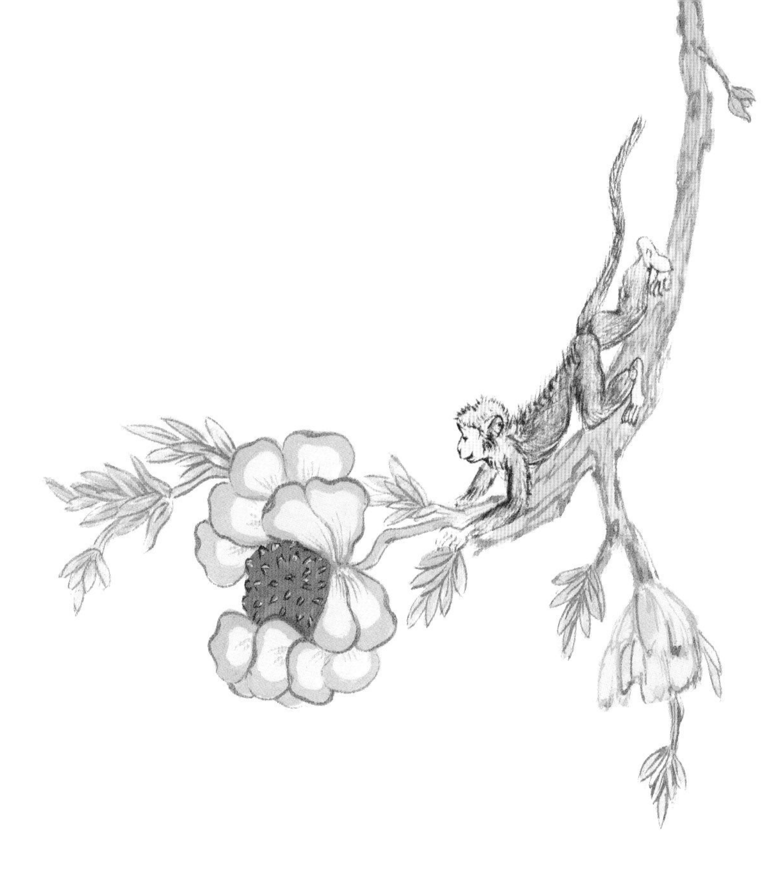

*Nirvana* The end of the Holy Paths
*Non-Reverting Bodhisattva* A bodhisattva who will not be bodily reborn
*Parinirvana* The death of the latest Buddha
*Pataliputra* The ancient capital of one of the kingdoms of northern India, now called Patna
*Perfection of Wisdom* Illumination
*Pindola* See Bharadvaja Pindola
*Prabhutaratna* A Buddha of ancient times
*Prostration* A ritual act of devotion
*Right Conduct* Conduct according to the Buddha's teaching
*Saha* This world
*Sakra* The king of the lower gods
*Sakyamuni* The name of the historical Buddha, meaning 'the sage of the Sakya clan'
*Samantabhadra* A great bodhisattva
*Samsara* The whole world according to Buddhism
*Sangha* Monks and nuns
*Sankasya* An ancient city in northern India
*Sariputra* An eminent arhat and one of the two chief disciples of the Buddha
*Sarvastivadin School* An early school of Indian Buddhism
*Sarvasughanda* A buddha-field whose name means 'Perfumed Land'
*Silk Road* An ancient trade route which ran from China, through Central Asia to the eastern Mediterranean, along which all kinds of goods travelled, including the transmission of the Buddhist teaching from India to China
*Sravasti* An ancient city in northern India
*Stupa* A religious monument
*Subhuti* An eminent arhat
*Sunyata* The idea that all things are insubstantial
*Sutra* A Buddhist scripture
*Swat* A river in northern Pakistan
*Taxila* A town in northern Pakistan
*the Path* A term used to describe various ways recommended by the different schools to attain final Buddhist goals
*Trisula* The three-pronged sceptre, which is the symbol of the 'three jewels' of the Buddha, the Dharma and the Sangha
*Universe of the Perfumed Garden* A state of consciousness
*Upagupta* An arhat
*Vaishali* An ancient city in northern India
*Vimalakirti* A mythical Indian Buddhist layman
*Vulture Peak* A mountain near the ancient city of Rajagriha in India
*Yasas* An early arhat disciple of the Buddha

# BIOGRAPHIES

## ERIC CHEETHAM

At the end of the last war (the Second World War) Eric Cheetham was discharged from operational flying in the RAF and found himself without a religion or a faith in anything and a very jaundiced view of himself and society. With the support of a few close friends, his search began for a valid and effective new ideal. Several years of intensive reading and research followed. At last, around the year 1950, he discovered the Dharma and his life began to change. In 1951 he joined The London Buddhist Society and shortly afterward Professor R. H. Robinson became the first of two teachers who opened up the wonders of the Mahayana to him. The second teacher was Dr. E. Conze. He formed a succession of study groups to explore the sutras and commentaries. After he had given a series of lectures and classes at several of the Buddhist Society's Summer Schools, he received invitations to mount and deliver two lecture series at the Buddhist Society; the first on Mainstream Buddhism and the second on Mahayana. The success of these courses resulted in both being published. Both before and after these major projects he continued his textual study. He gave a further series of talks given at the Buddhist Society over eighteen months in 1984 and 1985 which were developed into a volume on Chinese Buddhism published privately in 2013.

## ROBERTA MANSELL

After studying Fine Art and Philosophy in California, Roberta Mansell moved to England in 1961. Between 1962 and 1990 she taught art and illustration in schools and colleges and worked as a freelance illustrator. Since 1980 she has been a Zen trainee with Venerable Myokyo-ni and Martin Goodson at the Buddhist Society and the Zen Centre in London and the Hampshire Buddhist Society in Southampton.

Having heard of the Lotus Sutra from Eric Cheetham at the Buddhist Society Summer School, she started hand copying and illuminating the H. Kern translation in 1988. This project is expected to be completed in 2016.

Some of the illustrations for the Silk Road stories are from the *Illuminated Lotus Sutra* project.

# ACKNOWLEDGEMENTS

Firstly, we wish to thank the English and French translators of the sutras because without them there would be no stories. These stories are an ancient method of transmission in all the Buddhist countries from Sri Lanka through India to Tibet, South East Asia and the Far East.

We are grateful for the help and technical support of Roger Jarvis, Peter Glynne-Jones, Stuart Devlin, James Newell, Jonny Templeton, Avni Patel, Sarah Auld and Jonathan Earl.

Lastly, we thank the Hokun Trust and the Buddhist Society who made it all possible.